HOME ALONE™

Books by Todd Strasser

The Mall From Outer Space

The Complete Computer Popularity Program

Friends Till the End

The Wave

Ferris Bueller's Day Off

HOME ALONe™

A novelization by Todd Strasser
Based on the Screenplay by John Hughes

SCHOLASTIC INC.
New York Toronto London Auckland Sydney

ISBN 0-590-44668-1

12 11 10 9 8 7 1 2 3 4 5 6/9

Printed in the U.S.A. 40

First Scholastic printing, January 1991

To Michael, Andrea and Noah Strone

December 21
Oak Park, Illinois
6 P.M.

Kevin McCallister, aged seven, wandered through his house, looking for something to do. He was a thin boy, still waiting for a significant growth spurt. He had brown hair and almost all of his adult teeth.

Just about every room in the big old three-story brick house was being used by one McCallister or another. Kevin had counted fifteen of them — seven in his family and six in his Uncle Frank's family, and two cousins. And at the moment none of them wanted Kevin around because they were too busy packing clothes and wrapping gifts. Tomorrow morning they were all flying to France to spend Christmas in Paris.

"Hey, Kevin!" he heard Uncle Frank shout from the study. Frank and his family had arrived from Ohio that afternoon.

"What?" Kevin shouted back.

"Come help me with this VCR," Frank shouted.

Kevin wasn't sure he wanted to. Uncle Frank was the bald, chubby brother of Kevin's father, Peter McCallister. Sometimes Uncle Frank picked on Kevin. Still, Kevin had nothing better to do.

He went into the study and found Frank hunched over the VCR. Kevin's cousins Tracy and Heather were sitting on the couch. Tracy was Frank's daughter. She was blonde and had braces. Heather had brown hair and wore a Northwestern University sweatshirt. Her father and mother had moved to Paris the previous summer, which was why everyone was going there for Christmas. Tracy and Heather were teenagers.

Kevin quickly identified the problem with the VCR. "You've messed up all the channels, Uncle Frank. How come you don't know how to use a VCR?"

Tracy and Heather giggled. Uncle Frank glanced at the girls and then turned back to Kevin.

"How come you don't know how to drive?" he asked back.

"I'm not old enough to drive," Kevin said. "You're old enough to use a VCR."

"Two points!" Tracy shouted. She and Heather giggled again. Uncle Frank frowned.

"Think you're pretty smart for a seven-year-old, don't you?" he muttered. "Just get this to work, okay?"

Kevin turned the VCR and the TV back to the right channels and a movie went on. It was an old black-and-white gangster movie Uncle Frank had brought. Uncle Frank settled back into the sofa with the girls. Kevin started to leave, but then stopped behind the sofa. He'd never seen black-and-white TV before.

"Why did they make movies in black and white?" he asked.

"You still here?" Uncle Frank seemed surprised. "Get goin'."

"Why can't I watch?" Kevin asked.

"You're not old enough," Uncle Frank said.

"How come I'm old enough to fix the VCR, but not old enough to watch what's on it?" Kevin asked.

"I said get out of here!" Uncle Frank yelled.

"I'm telling my mother," Kevin yelled back.

"Great, just go."

Kevin went. Uncle Frank was a jerk.

The McCallister house was on a quiet street lined with tall old trees in the fancy Chicago suburb of Oak Park. The people who lived there tended to be well-off. They liked to travel during holidays like Christmas. The two crooks who sat in the dark van across from the McCallister house were counting on it.

"Just think," said Marv Murchens, gazing at the houses glimmering with colorful Christmas lights. "By tomorrow afternoon almost everyone on this block should be away." Marv was a tall, lanky man with a scruffy beard and a confused look on his face.

His partner, Harry Lyme, smiled and his gold tooth glinted. Harry was a short, heavyset man with cropped black hair and a mean scowl.

"See that house there?" Harry pointed at the McCallister house. "That's the one I really want. I bet it's loaded."

"You sure they're goin' away?" Marv asked.

"We better make sure," Harry said. He got up and went into the back of the van to change clothes.

"Yeah," Marv said. "No sense robbing the place if the people are home."

Back in the McCallister house, Kevin's mother Kate was in her bedroom, talking on the phone to her office while she packed a suitcase. With her dark wavy hair, black business suit, and glittering jewelry, she looked like a character from *Dynasty*. But then, she was a clothes designer and worked in the fashion business.

"I don't want any calls while I'm away," Kate was saying. "I'm not going to France so I can spend the holidays on the phone."

Kevin ran into the room. He knew his mother hated to be interrupted while she was on the phone, but he was mad at her because she hadn't taken him to Santa's Village that day to see Santa Claus. Besides, this was more important than some dumb phone call.

"Uncle Frank won't let me watch the movie," he shouted. "If the big kids can, why can't I?"

"Shush," Kate said. Then to the phone she said, "We put Ralphy in the kennel . . . what? No, Ralphy's the dog. I gave them the office number in case there's a problem."

"But Mom . . ." Kevin tugged at her dress. "It's not even an R movie. Uncle Frank's just being a jerk."

Kate put her hand over the phone. "If Frank said no, I say no."

"That's not fair," Kevin shouted, but his mother ignored him. Kevin saw that her dresses were laid out on the bed, waiting to be packed for the trip. He flopped down on the bed.

"Kevin!" Kate snapped. "Get off there!"

Kevin slid off the bed, making sure a few of his mom's dresses slid onto the floor, too. Kate's eyes widened with anger.

"Get out of here!" she shouted.

"Hang up the phone and make me," Kevin shouted back.

In the middle of this, Kevin's father Peter stepped out of the bathroom. He was a handsome man with short black hair. He'd just come home from the office, and was still wearing his business shirt and tie.

"Kate?" he said. "Where's the voltage adaptor thing?"

"I didn't have time to pick one up," Kate replied. "And I wish everyone would stop interrupting me when I'm on the phone."

"How am I gonna shave in France?" Peter asked.

Kate didn't answer. Kevin headed for his father. If he couldn't get his mother to say yes, maybe his dad would.

"Dad," he whined. "Nobody'll let me do anything."

"I'll let you do something," his father said. "Go pick up your Micromachines. Aunt Leslie stepped on one and nearly broke her neck."

"And I found him in the workroom before, fooling around with the blowtorch," Kate said from across the room.

Squealer, Kevin thought. Suddenly he decided it was time to leave.

"Wait a minute," his dad said sternly. "What have I told you about that? That torch is for grown-ups only. Never, ever play around with it."

"But Buzz showed me how," Kevin said.

Before his father could reply, Aunt Leslie came in. She was Uncle Frank's wife and chubby like him. She talked with a real squeaky voice.

"How come Uncle Frank won't let me — " Kevin began to ask, but Aunt Leslie held up her hand.

"In a minute, Kevin," she squeaked.

"*'In a minute, Kevin.'*" Kevin imitated Aunt Leslie's squeak.

"Kevin!" Peter shouted, glaring at his son. "Out! Right now!"

Kevin stuck out his tongue and left.

Harry Lyme stepped onto the McCallisters' front porch and rang the doorbell. The policeman's uniform he'd rented from the costume shop was tight around the neck and too short in the arms.

A blonde girl about fourteen years old opened the door. "Can I help you?" she asked.

"Yes, are your parents home?" Harry said, stepping into the foyer.

"Yeah, but they don't live here," Tracy replied.

Harry scowled. "Huh?"

Just then Heather passed by, lugging a suitcase.

"Hey, Tracy," she said. "Did you call for the pizzas?"

"Buzz did," Tracy answered. "By the way, my dad said an American hair dryer won't work in France. Is that true?"

France, thought Harry with a smile.

"You need a voltage adaptor," Heather told her.

"What's that?" Tracy asked.

"Ask your mom," Heather said.

"Excuse me," Harry said to Heather. "Are your parents here?"

"My parents live in Paris," Heather said. Now a younger girl with glasses joined them.

Big family, Harry thought, imagining all the TVs they must have.

"*Bonjour*, Mr. Policeman," the younger girl said.

"Wrong, Sondra," Heather said. "*Bonjour* means good day. It's evening now."

"Hi," Harry said to Sondra, "are your parents home?"

"*Oui*," said Sondra.

"Do they live here?" Harry asked.

"No," said Sondra.

"If you'll wait here a minute I'll try to find someone," Heather told Harry. Then she, Tracy and Sondra left.

Harry looked around at the expensive-looking furniture in the living room. He could almost bet the cabinet in the dining room was filled with sterling silver and valuable china. Harry grinned. This was going to be a great house to rob.

DECEMBER 21
OAK PARK
6:30 P.M.

Kevin stood in front of the upstairs hallway closet and stared up at the suitcase on the top shelf. He was supposed to pack for this dumb trip to France, but there was no way he could reach his suitcase.

Just then his sister Megan came by. Megan had curly brown hair and spent a lot of time in the bathroom. She was a teenager, and considerably taller than he.

"Hey, Megan," Kevin said. "Help me get my suitcase?"

"Get it yourself," said Megan. "I have to use the bathroom."

"But I can't reach it," Kevin said.

"Tough." Megan walked away.

Kevin sighed. It wasn't easy being the youngest kid in the family. He'd heard all this stuff about how great it was to be the "baby" and how everyone spoiled you. But forget it. To him being the youngest just meant being the first to get dumped on.

Kevin went into the room he shared with his brother Jeff, who was nine, and wasn't a teenager but looked and acted like he was. Jeff even lifted weights. At that moment he was lifting a big green duffle bag.

"There, I'm packed," Jeff said proudly. "Have you packed?"

"I can't reach my suitcase," Kevin said. "And even if I could, I don't know how to pack. I've never done it in my whole life."

"You've never done anything in your whole life," Jeff sneered. "Except play piano . . . badly."

"I'm only seven," Kevin said.

"Tough," said Jeff.

"That's what Megan said," Kevin sighed.

"What did I say?" asked Megan as she passed on her way back from the bathroom.

"You told Kevin 'tough,' " said Jeff.

"The dope was whining about a suitcase," Megan said. "What am I supposed to do? Shake his hand and say, 'Congratulations, you're an idiot?' "

"I'm not an idiot!" Kevin shouted.

"Oh, really," Megan said with a laugh. "You're completely helpless. Everybody has to do everything for you."

Kevin glared at Megan, who went back to her room. Now his sister Linnie stuck her head into the bedroom. Linnie had long straight blonde hair and was beautiful. She was twelve and almost a teenager. That's the way life was for Kevin. Everyone in his family was a teenager, or almost a teenager, or acted like a teenager. Everyone except him.

"I hope you didn't just pack junk, Jeff," Linnie said.

"Shut up," replied Jeff.

"Do you know what I should pack?" Kevin asked her.

"Didn't Buzz tell you, cheekface?" Jeff said as he lugged his duffle bag out of the room. "Toilet paper and water."

As soon as Jeff left the room, Kevin stuck his tongue out at him.

"Don't worry." Linnie patted Kevin on the head. "You know Mom's going to pack your stuff. You're what the French call *les incompetent.*"

"Thanks," Kevin sniffed.

"You know you have to sleep on the hide-a-bed with Fuller tonight," Linnie said.

"Why?" Kevin asked. Fuller was Kevin's five-year-old cousin. He wasn't a teenager, but he was Uncle Frank's kid so he didn't count.

"Heather, Tracy and Sondra have to sleep in your room," Linnie said. "Don't forget. If Fuller has a Pepsi he wets his bed."

Kevin clenched his fist. *This was the final hu-*

miliation! Not only did they treat him worse than Ralphy the dog, but they were taking his room away and making him sleep with a bed wetter!

"This house is so full of people, it makes me sick," Kevin shouted. "When I grow up and get married, I'm living alone!"

Linnie started to laugh. Kevin wondered why.

Harry Lyme was still standing in the foyer in his phony police uniform. Twenty-five minutes had passed. By now he'd surveyed everything and figured the take on this place would be in the thousands of dollars. If only he could find out when, and if, everyone was going to France.

The doorbell rang. From upstairs someone yelled, "Get the door!" Harry was the only one close to the door so he figured that meant him. He opened it. A Little Nero's Pizza delivery boy came in trying to balance a huge stack of pizza boxes.

"It comes to a hundred twenty-two dollars, sir," the kid said, trying to hand Harry the receipt.

"Sorry," said Harry. "But I don't live here."

"Just here for the holidays?" the pizza boy asked.

"Yeah, in a way," Harry said with a smile.

Someone upstairs yelled "Bombs away!" and a green duffle bag crashed to the floor near Harry.

"Hope you live through it," said the delivery boy.

A fat bald guy came down the stairs. Harry wondered if he was the man of the house. "Excuse me, sir," Harry said. "If I could just — "

"In a minute," Frank said as he took the pizza boxes. "We have an important transaction to accomplish first."

"Yeah, it's a hundred and twenty-two bucks," said the pizza boy.

"My brother'll get it. This is his house," said Frank. Then he turned toward the stairs and shouted, "Pizza's here!"

A stampede of kids emerged from every corner of the house, followed by a chubby lady.

"Excuse me, ma'am," Harry said, smoothing his hair back. "Are you Mrs. McCallister?"

"Yes," squeaked Aunt Leslie, "but I'm not the Mrs. McCallister who lives here." She went into the kitchen.

"I don't know about you," the pizza delivery boy said to Harry, "but I'm not leaving without my money."

Harry just smiled. With any luck, he'd be back for his tomorrow.

December 21
Oak Park
6:45 p.m.

Kevin didn't hear Uncle Frank's call for pizza because he was in Buzz's room. Buzz was his big brother and he always played his Guns n' Roses tape loud. Buzz was a real teenager with big muscles and a three-inch waxed flattop.

Buzz's room had posters of Bo Jackson and Axl Rose on the walls, and all kinds of weights and baseball gloves and football equipment lying around. On one of Buzz's shelves were a dozen ceramic figurines of famous sports heros like Don Mattingly and Joe Montana.

At that moment Kevin was sitting in the corner because Buzz had told him to sit there and not speak until Buzz gave him permission. Meanwhile Buzz was packing a suitcase and talking to their cousin Rod. Rod was kind of skinny and had pimples. Kevin had heard Megan call Rod a nerd behind his back.

Right now Rod was looking in a glass terrarium at Buzz's pet tarantula, Axl.

"Who's gonna feed your spider while you're gone?" Rod asked.

"He just had a bunch of mice guts," Buzz said. "That should hold him till we get back."

Kevin wondered if Buzz would let him speak now, but Buzz had something else on his mind.

"Hey, Rod," he said. "Is it true that French babes don't shave their pits?"

"Some don't," Rod said.

"And they go to nude beaches?" asked Buzz.

"Not in the winter," said Rod.

"Darn," said Buzz.

Kevin raised his hand.

"Did I tell you to raise your hand?" Buzz barked.

"I have a question," Kevin said.

"Okay, what?" Buzz sighed.

"Can I sleep in your room tonight?" Kevin asked. "I don't wanna sleep in the family room with Fuller because if he has a Pepsi he wets the bed."

"I wouldn't let you sleep in my room if you were growing on my arm," Buzz snapped. He was about to tell Kevin to get lost when he noticed something outside his window.

"Hey, check this out." Buzz pressed his face against the glass. "It's old man Marley."

Kevin felt a shiver of fright. Old man Marley had stringy white hair and a scraggly beard and lived across the street. He wore tattered clothes, shuffled with a limp, and always carried a snow shovel. Just the thought of him made Kevin want to hide in his mother's bed. But he decided to be brave and listen to what Buzz told Rod.

"Who is he?" Rod asked, joining Buzz at the window.

"Ever heard of the South Bend Shovel Slayer?" Buzz asked.

"No."

"Well that's him," said Buzz. "About thirty years ago he murdered his whole family and half the people on his block with a snow shovel. He's been hiding out in this neighborhood ever since."

"If he's the slayer," Rod said, "how come the cops don't arrest him?"

"Lack of evidence," Buzz said. "They never found the bodies. But everyone around here knows he did it. It's just a matter of time before he does it again."

Buzz turned and gave Kevin a scary look. "Right, Kev?"

Kevin backed into the corner and didn't answer.

"What's he doing?" Rod asked, pointing out the window. Marley was standing at the street curb, using the shovel to clear a clogged sewer grate.

"It's hard to say," Buzz answered, glancing back at Kevin. "Probably psyching himself up for another killing spree."

"Maybe he dumps the bodies in the sewer," Rod said.

"Naw, he's just trying to fake people out. He hides the bodies in his basement," Buzz said. He turned to Kevin. "You know all those mannequins Mom keeps in our basement?"

Kevin nodded.

"I bet Marley's basement looks just like that," said Buzz. "Except instead of mannequins, they're . . . real . . . dead . . . bodies!"

Kevin's eyes went wide. That was it! He'd heard enough! He was going to find Mom! He ran out the door . . . and ran right into his father. Kevin grabbed his father's leg and held tight. Back in the room, Buzz and Rod were laughing.

Why did everyone laugh? Kevin wondered.

"You look like you've seen a ghost," Peter said. Kevin just trembled. Peter stuck his head into Buzz's room. "If you played the music lower you'd know the pizza's here."

"Pizza!" Buzz shouted. He and Rod burst out of the room. Peter looked down at Kevin, who was still clinging to his leg.

"Hey, there's nothing to be scared of," Peter said.

Kevin shrugged and held tighter to his father's leg.

"I'm looking forward to the day when you're as big as Buzz," Peter said.

"So am I," answered Kevin.

Harry looked at his watch. It was going on forty-five minutes and he still hadn't spoken to an actual responsible head of the household. Two teenagers had recently run past, but neither looked very responsible. Next to him the pizza boy was getting impatient.

"Don't they know time is money?" he asked.

I've got the time, Harry thought, looking around. And they've got the money.

A responsible-looking gentleman now started down the stairs, accompanied by a little kid.

"Excuse me," Harry said. "Are you the Mr. McCallister who actually lives here?"

"Uh, yes," said Peter.

"Great," the pizza boy cut in before Harry could continue. "Because someone owes me a hundred-and-twenty-two bucks."

Kevin stared up at Harry in wonder. He'd never seen a gold tooth before. Harry noticed the kid staring at him funny. It gave him the creeps, but he had to keep up the charade.

"And I need a word with you, sir," Harry said.

"My wife will be down in a second," Peter said. "She'll take care of both of you."

Peter and Kevin left. For the first time that evening Harry didn't mind being left alone. He was glad to get rid of that kid.

December 21
Oak Park
7 PM

By the time Kevin got to the kitchen, there were open pizza boxes all over the place. Everyone was taking slices and cups of soda.

"Use paper plates, everyone!" Aunt Leslie squeaked. "And don't give Fuller any Pepsi."

Kevin grabbed a plate and headed for the nearest pizza box, but Uncle Frank put out a fat hand and stopped him. "*Parlez-vous français* yet, squirt?"

Everyone stopped talking and stared at Kevin.

"My name isn't squirt," he said. "It's Kevin."

"Yeah?" said Frank. "Know what they're gonna call you in France?"

"What?" asked Kevin.

Frank reached around his waist and grabbed

hold of his pants. "Yank!" Uncle Frank shouted, yanking down Kevin's pants. Everyone laughed. Kevin quickly pulled up his pants. He was so angry he wanted to punch Uncle Frank in his fat face. But he was hungry so he went for the pizza instead. In the meantime everyone started talking again.

"What time do we have to go to bed?" little Fuller asked, his face smeared red with pizza sauce.

"Early," said Uncle Frank, *his* face also smeared with pizza sauce. "We're leaving at nine A.M. On the button."

"I heard on the news there's a cold front moving in accompanied by high winds," Aunt Leslie squeaked. "I hope the planes aren't delayed."

"Are we taking the cars to the airport?" Heather asked.

"No, the airport limos are going to pick us up," said Peter. "It's cheaper than leaving three cars in long-term parking."

Kevin wasn't listening. The first pizza box was on the kitchen counter, stuck in among the family passports and a plastic half-gallon milk container. He looked inside, but it was empty. As Kevin headed for the next box his mother came into the kitchen.

"Is everyone drinking up the milk?" she asked. "I want to use it up so it doesn't go bad while we're away."

"Does Santa have to go through customs?"

asked Kevin's cousin Brooke, who was six and still sucked her thumb. No one answered her. Peter waved at Kate.

"Honey? The pizza boy needs a hundred and twenty-two bucks," he said.

"For pizza?" Kate looked shocked.

"Ten pizzas times twelve bucks," Uncle Frank said, trying to be helpful.

"Frank?" squeaked Aunt Leslie. "You have money, don't you?"

"Uh, it's all in traveler's checks," Frank said. He popped open a can of Pepsi and poured it into Fuller's glass.

"It's okay, we have cash," Kate said.

By now Kevin had searched all ten pizza boxes. It seemed as if the impossible had occurred.

"Didn't anyone order me a plain cheese pizza?" he asked.

"Yeah," said Buzz, his mouth packed with pizza. "But if you want any, somebody's gonna have to barf theirs up because it's all gone."

Kevin glared at Buzz. The girls at the table were giggling. Laughing at me, Kevin thought. All they do is laugh at me.

"Hey, Kevin, got a plate?" Buzz asked. Then he opened his mouth and crossed his eyes like he was going to barf.

The girls giggled louder. Kevin felt his cheeks start to burn. That was it! *That was just it!* Kevin charged Buzz and knocked his plate of pizza slices off the table. As Buzz lunged to catch the slices his elbow hit the plastic milk container on the counter. Milk spilled all over the family's passports.

"The passports!" Peter shouted, jumping up to grab them.

Kevin felt someone grab him, too. It was his mother.

"Napkins," Aunt Leslie was squealing. "Get napkins!"

Everyone was shouting. Uncle Frank slipped and got milk all over his shirt. Peter was holding the passports over the sink, letting the milk drip off them. Kevin tried to fight his way out of his mother's grip, but she held on tight and started to shake him angrily.

"What's the matter with you?" she shouted.

"He started it!" Kevin pointed at Buzz. "He ate my pizza on purpose. He knows I hate sausage and onions and — "

"Look what you did, you little jerk!" Uncle Frank shouted, holding out his wet shirt.

"You get upstairs!" Kate yelled and shook Kevin. "Right this minute!"

"Why?" Kevin shouted back.

"Because you're a disease!" yelled Tracy.

"Shut up!" Kevin yelled at her.

"Get upstairs!" Peter yelled.

Kevin felt his mother yank him by the collar out of the kitchen. He hated them. Every single one!

* * *

"Sounds like a real war," said the pizza boy. Harry nodded and looked at his watch. He was gonna have a war of his own if he didn't get back to Marv in the van pretty soon.

Just then an attractive lady came toward them dragging that creepy kid. Harry smoothed his hair back.

"I'm so sorry you had to wait," Kate told the pizza boy. With one hand she kept a firm hold on Kevin. With the other she handed the boy the pizza money.

"Nice tip," said the pizza boy. "Have a merry Christmas." He left.

"Uh, ma'am," Harry said, trying to sound super polite.

Kate turned to him. She had a lot on her mind and couldn't deal with anything extra right now. "Look, I'm awfully sorry," she said, "but if it's for some police charity I'm afraid this just isn't the right time. We're all going out of town tomorrow and it's just crazy around here. My husband's brother was transferred to Paris during the summer and his daughter goes to college here and his son is finishing high school and is staying with my brother-in-law."

"I understand," Harry said. "I just — "

"So as a Christmas present," Kate continued, "my husband's brother gave us a trip to Paris so we can all be together for the holidays. Anyway we're leaving for Paris in the morning . . ."

"No kidding?" Harry smiled. "All of you? How nice."

"Yes," said Kate. "And I realize that not everyone is fortunate enough to go to Paris for the holidays and . . . oh . . . it's Christmastime, what am I saying?"

Still holding on to Kevin's collar, she reached into her bag and came up with twenty dollars.

"Here," she said, handing the money to Harry. "May you and the police department have a merry Christmas."

"Uh, thanks, Mrs. McCallister." Harry stared down at the bills in his hand.

But Kate was already dragging Kevin upstairs. "And now I'm going to have a word with you."

Harry let himself out of the house and strolled across the lawn toward the van, loosening the collar on his fake police uniform. As he pulled open the door of the van he noticed that Marv was sitting in the driver's seat, shivering.

"Why didn't you keep the heat on?" Harry asked.

"Cause the carbon monoxide seeps in when you just sit," Marv said through chattering teeth. "So it was either die of carbon monoxide poisoning or freeze to death. Now how about telling me why you took so long?"

"They're crazy in there," said Harry. "But the

good news is tomorrow morning they're all going to Paris."

"All of 'em?" Marv asked.

"Yeah. So now we know five families on this block are gonna be gone for the holidays," Harry said. "Only that weird guy Marley's gonna be around and he looks pretty flaky to me."

"So we can rob houses and there'll be no one around to notice," Marv said happily.

"And let me tell you," said Harry, feeling the twenty dollars in his pocket. "That McCallister house is gonna be a good one."

DECEMBER 21
OAK PARK
7:30 P.M.

Kate was at her wit's end. "It's getting late," she told Kevin angrily. "We're leaving for Paris first thing in the morning and you're driving everyone crazy."

"You're all driving me crazy," Kevin yelled back.

Kate pulled him into the upstairs hallway. She took a breath and tried to control her temper. The truth was, she hated punishing any of her kids. If Kevin would just say he was sorry and start to act like a human being instead of a spoiled brat, she would be happy to let him go.

"Now listen to me, young man," she said sternly. "There are fifteen people in this house. And you're the only one who has to make trouble."

"I'm the only one getting picked on," Kevin wailed.

"You're the only one acting up," Kate snapped back, feeling her blood begin to boil. "Now get upstairs."

"I *am* upstairs, dummy."

That was it! Kate had never felt angrier. How had this . . . this monster come into their family? There must've been a mistake at the hospital. Babies were switched or something. Anyway, she knew what she had to do.

"Come with me," she said, grabbing him by the collar.

"Where?" Kevin gasped.

"You know where." Kate pulled open the door at the end of the hallway. A narrow flight of stairs led up to the attic. Kevin's eyes grew large.

"The attic?" he whimpered.

"Go!" Kate pointed up the stairs. Kevin looked up into the attic. It was dark and empty. There were noises up there.

"It's scary, Mom." His voice was filled with pleading, but Kate's was filled with resolve.

"You should have thought of that before you lost your temper," she scolded.

"I'm sorry," Kevin whispered. He thought about throwing himself at her feet and begging for mercy.

"It's too late for that," Kate said firmly. "Now go."

Kevin pursed his lips together angrily. The remorseful approach wasn't going to work.

"Everybody in this family hates me!" he shouted.

"Then maybe you should ask Santa Claus for a new family," his mother suggested.

"I don't want a new family," Kevin cried as he climbed the first step. "I don't want any family! Families stink!"

"Go!" his mother shouted. "And you stay up there. I don't want to see you for the rest of the night!"

Kevin took another step. "I don't want to ever see you again for the rest of my life and I don't want to see anybody else either!"

Kate watched her angry little boy climb up the steps. She felt a strange mixture of frustration and heartache.

"I hope you don't mean that," she said. "You'd feel pretty sad if you woke up tomorrow and we were all gone."

"No, I wouldn't," Kevin said, and slammed the attic door. "I hope I never see any of you jerks again!"

December 22
Oak Park
3:15 a.m.

That night strong gusts of cold wind blew through the Chicago area. On Kevin's street the trees swayed and branches rattled, Christmas decorations blew over and a plastic Santa tumbled across a yard. Broken twigs clattered against the roof of the McCallister house, waking Kevin in the attic.

Kevin sat up. He was still angry. He'd show them. He'd run away. He looked across the shadowy attic at the big metal hook and escape rope near the window. His father kept the rope in case there was a fire and someone had to escape by crawling out onto the roof and lowering himself down. That's what he'd do. He'd crawl out the window, lower himself to the oak tree next to the house, and hide all night in his tree house.

Tomorrow morning when his mother couldn't find him, she'd think he'd run away. That would teach her to put him in the attic.

But Kevin didn't move. The wind and noises outside scared him. The thought of spending the night in his tree house was scary, too. And so was the idea of climbing out the attic window. Kevin sighed and looked at the attic door. He wasn't going to show them anything. And all he did when he tried to show them was get into more trouble. Why did he have to say such mean things? He knew it just hurt his mother's feelings. What good did that do?

It did no good at all. All it meant was now he had to spend the night in this scary attic.

Kevin lay down again and shut his eyes. Outside the wind blew even louder. Somewhere in the night a loose shutter banged. A few doors down from the McCallisters', a large branch on a tall elm snapped and fell across the telephone and power lines, bringing them down with a shower of sparks.

In every house on Kevin's side of the street the refrigerators shut off, the burglar alarms deactivated and the electric clocks stopped. Including the alarm clock beside Peter and Kate McCallister's bed.

DECEMBER 22
OAK PARK
9 A.M.

Kate McCallister was dreaming about Paris. She and Peter were in an elegant hotel suite overlooking the Seine. The French doors to the balcony were open and fragrant French air billowed in. Room service had just left a tray of *café au lait*, fresh croissants and assorted jams. . . .

But someone was knocking loudly on their hotel room door.

Why are they knocking so loudly? Kate wondered in her dream. She rolled over in her bed. The dream slowly disappeared, but the knocking didn't. *Bang! Bang! Bang!*

"Hello!?" someone shouted outside. "Is anyone there? It's the airport limo!"

Kate's eyes opened. Airport limo? Oh no! She

sat straight up in bed and stared at the alarm clock. 3:17? It couldn't be. It was light outside. Downstairs the banging and shouting continued.

"The electricity must've gone off during the night," Kate gasped as she shook Peter's shoulder. She grabbed her wristwatch from the night table. The big hand was on the 12. The little hand was on the 9. Peter rubbed his eyes.

"Hurry!" Kate said. "We're late!"

Seconds later Kate was pulling on her robe and flying through the house like a maniac, shouting and banging on doors as she went.

"Wake up! Everybody, up, up!" She got to the front door and told the two van drivers her family was running a little behind schedule, but they'd be right down. There were two other vans parked out on the street. One was from Commonwealth Power and Light. The other was from the OHKAY Heating and Plumbing Company. But Kate didn't have time to wonder about that now.

In bedrooms all over the house people hurriedly dressed and grabbed their bags. Kate ran back upstairs to dress herself. Heather was coming down the stairs and Kate grabbed her.

"Heather, you have to do a head count. Make sure everyone's in the vans," Kate said. Then she saw Peter lugging their suitcases out onto the upstairs landing.

"Have you got the tickets and the passports?" Kate shouted.

"I thought you had 'em," Peter shouted back.

"I have them!" Aunt Leslie squeaked.

"Yours or ours?" Kate shouted.

"All of them," Aunt Leslie squeaked back. "I know because they smell of sour milk."

As sleepy-faced kids began to file out of the house, dragging their bags across the lawn to the airport vans, it attracted the attention of little Mitch Murphy, who lived in the house next door. Mitch was seven years old and about the same size as Kevin. In a few hours he and his parents would be leaving for Orlando, Florida. But Mitch had some time to kill and the airport vans looked neat.

"These vans are cool," Mitch said as he wandered over and watched the van drivers hastily load luggage inside.

"No way on earth we're gonna catch that plane," Uncle Frank wheezed as he came out of the house with a suitcase.

"Think positive," said Peter.

Mitch stuck his head in one of the vans. He'd never seen one so long. You could get a whole baseball team inside.

"Frank?" Aunt Leslie was shouting. "Do you have the money?"

"Darn," Frank mumbled and jogged back inside. "I left it upstairs."

"Come on, everyone," Heather shouted. "Line up so I can get a count."

The kids gathered beside the van. Mitch Murphy was there too, looking inside. Cool dashboard, he thought.

"One, two, three, four . . ." Heather quickly began to count the kids, including Mitch, whose back was turned so she couldn't see his face.

"Ninety-three, six hundred and five, elevendy-trillion," Buzz yelled.

"Don't be a moron, Buzz," Heather snapped. She finished the head count. Everyone was there. "Okay, get in! Half in this van, half in the other."

The kids all climbed into the vans. Mitch Murphy turned around and headed back to his house. A moment later Kate locked the front door and ran toward the lead van.

"Heather!" she gasped. "You counted everyone?"

"Eleven kids including me," Heather replied. "Six girls, five boys, four parents, two drivers and a partridge in a pear tree."

"Great!" said Kate. She was just about to climb into the airport van when the man from Commonwealth Power and Light came by. He was wearing a blue hard hat.

"Excuse me, ma'am," he said.

"I'm sorry," Kate said quickly as she got into the van. "But I'm really in a rush. I have a plane to catch."

"I just wanted to say that the power's fixed," the man said. "But the phone lines were torn up real bad. It'll probably take the phone company a couple of days to fix your phones. . . ."

But the airport van was already rolling down the driveway.

Across the street in the OHKAY Heating and Plumbing van, Marv and Harry watched the two airport vans speed away. Harry grinned and his gold tooth glinted.

"Four down, one family to go," he said. "As soon as the Murphys leave for Florida, the block is ours. I keep thinking about all that money, all those greenbacks."

"Yeah," grinned Marv. Then he started to sing, "I'm dreaming of a green Christmas!"

Someone else was dreaming, too. In the McCallisters' attic, Kevin jerked and groaned as he dreamed of all the body parts in old man Marley's basement. Arms and legs and heads laying around with bugs and rats crawling in and out of them. . . .

Kevin lurched out of his sleep. He rubbed his eyes and looked around. For once he was glad to be in the attic. Anything was better than old man Marley's basement. Kevin got up. He'd gone to bed the previous night without dinner and he was hungry.

He let himself out of the attic and used the bathroom, then went down to the kitchen. No one was there yet so he turned on the counter TV and watched Road Runner cartoons. As soon as his mom came down he was going to ask her for bacon and eggs and toast. Kevin scratched his ear and yawned. Where was she anyway? It sure seemed quiet in the house this morning.

December 22
O'Hare Airport
Chicago 10 A.M.

Miraculously, the McCallisters made it to the airport just in time to board the 747 bound for Paris. The four adults sat in the first-class section. The kids sat in coach. Peter and Kate were still trying to catch their breaths as the jet took off with a roar and nosed its way up into the sky.

"I can't believe we made it," Kate sighed happily.

"Hey, it's Christmas," Peter whispered, squeezing her hand. "The time for miracles."

"It'll be a miracle if we make it all the way to France without being bothered by those kids," muttered Frank. He and Leslie were sitting across the aisle.

"Did the kids get settled okay?" Kate asked.

"They only had single seats left in coach," Peter said. "They're okay, just spread out."

"Do you think it's right to sit in first class while the kids fly coach?" Aunt Leslie asked.

"When I was a kid we didn't even fly coach," Frank grumbled. "We flew station wagon. And it wasn't to France either. Those kids'll be fine. Don't worry."

Kate tried to relax, but something was nagging at her. Peter noticed that she was fidgeting.

"Hey, what is it?" he asked.

"I don't know." Kate tried to shrug it off.

"Come on, be happy," Peter said. "Not only did we make the flight, but we're headed for Paris."

"I know." Kate smiled weakly. "There's just something bothering me. I can't put my finger on it. It's probably something silly like rushing out and leaving the beds unmade."

December 22
Oak Park
10:15 A.M.

Kevin could've watched the Road Runner bash Wile E. Coyote all day, but his stomach was starting to growl. Everyone must've stayed up real late last night because there wasn't a sound in the house. Kevin frowned. That was so typical. They all stayed up and had a good time while he had to go to bed.

He decided to go upstairs and wake his parents. If they wouldn't let him stay up late at night, there was no way he'd let them sleep late in the morning.

A moment later Kevin stepped into his parents' bedroom. The bed was empty and unmade.

"Mom? Dad?" he called. No one answered.

He looked in the bathroom and back out in the hall.

"Hey, where are you guys?" Again, no one answered.

Kevin decided to ask Buzz. He'd know where their parents were. But Buzz's bedroom was empty. So was Megan's and his own. Soon Kevin had worked his way through the whole house. Every room was empty.

"I know! They're in the basement, playing a trick on me."

Kevin ran downstairs and burst through the basement door. It was dark and shadowy.

"Dad? Mom? Megan? Buzz? Aunt Leslie? Uncle Frank?" Kevin called out all their names, but no one answered. Where were those dumb people?

Then Kevin remembered . . . France! They were all supposed to go to France today! A terrible thought struck him. Could they have gone without him?

Kevin raced to the garage and looked inside. Relief! His parents' cars were there. And Uncle Frank's car was still parked in the driveway. So they couldn't have gone to the airport.

But if they weren't gone and they weren't here, where were they? Kevin went back into the kitchen. The red light on the coffeemaker was glowing. His mother always made sure it was off before she went out. She always made the beds, too. Kevin's eye drifted to the pile of empty pizza boxes. And his mom always, *always*, made sure the garbage was thrown —

Kevin gasped, remembering the fight over the pizza the night before. He'd wished his family would disappear! Could it be? Was it possible?

"I made my family disappear," Kevin whispered. But as he thought of his family, he remembered that Megan had called him an idiot, Linnie said he was *les incompetent*, Tracy said he was a disease, Uncle Frank called him a jerk and had pulled down his pants. And now he was supposed to feel bad for those dorks? No way. A small smile appeared on his face. This could be great!

In the OHKAY Plumbing and Heating van, Harry and Marv watched the Murphys pack up their station wagon and drive away. Harry leaned back in his seat.

"Okay," he said with a satisfied grin. "They're all gone and none of 'em will be back until after Christmas. And the great part is they told me from their own mouths."

"It's almost too easy," Marv said.

"Remember the old days?" Harry asked, lighting the butt of a half-smoked cigar. "Everybody stayed home for the holidays."

"Now it's off to Hawaii, Aspen, Paris," Marv said. "Whatever happened to sittin' around the fireplace with your family, roastin' chestnuts and singin' Christmas carols?"

"People have become cynical," Harry said,

shaking his head. "Everyone's too jaded. It's just another sign of the moral decay of contemporary society."

"Yeah," Marv nodded. "So which house you wanna rob first?"

December 22
Somewhere Over the Atlantic
11 A.M.

Kate still couldn't shake the feeling that something wasn't right. Here I am, sitting in first class, she thought. Going on a wonderful family vacation. Why should I feel like this?

"What is it, honey?" Peter asked.

"I don't know," Kate said. "I have this terribly anxious feeling."

"About what?" Peter asked.

"That we didn't do something," Kate said.

"It's just that we left in a hurry." Peter slid his arm around her shoulders and tried to reassure her. "I'm sure we took care of everything."

"Did I turn off the coffee machine?" Kate asked.

"I'm almost certain I did," said Peter.

"And we locked the house?" Kate said.

"Absolutely."

"You put the timers on the lights?" Kate asked.

"Check," said Peter with a smile. "And I closed the garage door."

"Did we put the answering machine on?" Kate asked.

"That's it!" Peter said. "Honey, I forgot. But look at it this way. We won't have to listen to all those dumb messages when we get home. And anyone with something important will call again."

Kate nodded.

"Do you feel better?" Peter asked. "Now that we know what it is?"

But Kate shook her head. "That wasn't it."

"I don't get it," said Peter. "What else could it be?"

DECEMBER 22
OAK PARK
11:30 A.M.

Munching on a bag of popcorn he'd just nuked in the microwave, Kevin stepped back into Buzz's room. This was great, just great! He could get his revenge on everyone. He could do whatever he pleased.

"Hey, Buzz," he shouted gleefully. "I'm in your room and I'm gonna go through all your private stuff! You better come out and pound me! Nah nah!"

He knew that Buzz kept a secret suitcase under his bed with all kinds of cool stuff in it. Kevin crawled under and pulled the suitcase out.

"Oh, cool!" he whispered as he opened it and found a whole mat of firecrackers and a box of BBs. Whoa! Kevin thought. What does Buzz need these for . . . unless he has a BB gun!

Kevin jumped up and looked around. Their parents didn't allow them to play with guns, but Buzz must've snuck one in. Good old Buzz. Kevin looked up at the bookcases on the wall. A little piece of brown plastic was visible on the highest shelf. Kevin climbed up on his brother's desk to get a better look. There it was! The BB gun and a tin baseball-card box.

Kevin opened the box. Inside were some $10 and $20 bills.

"Forget the money," Kevin whispered, closing the box and grabbing the gun. "It's time for target practice!"

Out in the hall Kevin lined up all of Buzz's sports figurines on the edge of the laundry chute. Then he walked to the opposite wall and picked up the BB gun.

"For the crime of belonging to my rashy brother and allowing yourself to be displayed in the pigsty he calls his room," Kevin announced. "I sentence you to death by BB wounds and falling all the way down the laundry chute to the creepy basement, where you'll die of massive head injuries."

Kevin aimed the BB gun at Don Mattingly. *POW!* Don Mattingly's head flew off and his body fell into the chute. *POW! POW!* He got Magic Johnson in the knee and shoulder. *POW!* Joe Montana sustained a severe stomach wound.

"This is the life," Kevin said with a smile.

* * *

Two houses away Harry and Marv carried armloads of stolen goods to their van.

"It was nice of these people to give their Christmas gifts before they went away," Marv said as he carried a brand-new Sony Trinitron TV set.

"Yeah," said Harry, who was carrying a Panasonic laser disc player. "Real considerate."

"So you want to get the house next door?" Marv asked.

"Naw," said Harry. "All this work makes me hungry. Let's break for lunch and hit it this afternoon."

DECEMBER 22
SOMEWHERE OVER THE ATLANTIC
3 P.M.

"Honey, you have to calm down," Peter said softly. "You're driving yourself crazy with worry over nothing."

"It's killing me, Peter." Kate was wracked with anxiety. She'd never felt this way before. All around her seat were little pieces of napkin she'd nervously torn up.

"But we've been over and over it," Peter said. "Everything's fine. We're here. The kids are here — "

Kate's eyes went wide. She jumped up and dashed through the curtain into the coach section.

"Kate, wait!" Peter followed her. "What's wrong?"

Kate stared at the rows of passengers. The

plane was full and most of them were reading or sleeping, but a few stared back at her. Kate searched for a familiar face and saw Megan.

"Megan, where's Kevin?"

"Uh, I think he's sitting over there," said Megan. "No, maybe he's behind me."

Kate moved down the aisle, staring at the faces. Fuller, Sondra, Jeff . . . but no Kevin.

"Heather!"

Startled, Heather looked up from a magazine. "Yes?"

"Where's Kevin?" Kate gasped.

"Uh, uh," Heather looked around. "I don't know."

In no time Kate had worked her way to the smoking section. Kevin wouldn't be back here, would he? She didn't see him anywhere.

Kate reached the back of the plane. All the bathrooms said "Unoccupied," but she checked them anyway. They were empty.

"Oh, no!" she gasped. "Oh, no!"

A stewardess in the rear galley scowled at her. "Can I help you?" she asked.

Suddenly the words burst out of Kate's mouth. *"STOP THE PLANE!"*

December 22
Oak Park
4:30 p.m.

Twelve dead sports figurines lay in a laundry basket in the basement. Kevin was in the family room watching the tape Uncle Frank wouldn't let him watch last night. A half-gallon container of chocolate fudge swirl was sitting on the coffee table, the ice cream inside slowly melting. Kevin dipped his spoon into it. He liked his ice cream soft.

On the TV a big gangster with scars on his face was standing in an apartment, talking through a door.

"Who is it?" the gangster asked.

"It's me, Snakes," someone answered. "I got the stuff."

"Leave it on the doorstep and get outa here," the gangster snapped.

"All right, Johnny. But what about my money?" the guy on the other side of the door asked.

"What money?" the gangster snarled.

"Acey said you'd have some dough for me."

"Is that a fact?" asked the gangster, picking up a machine gun. "How much do I owe you?"

Kevin hit the "hold" button on the remote and had another spoonful of ice cream. This movie wasn't so scary. Uncle Frank was just dumb.

"Hey, Uncle Frank!" Kevin shouted happily. "Hey, the rest of you guys! I'm watching rubbish and eating junk! You better stop me! Nah, nah!"

Kevin hit the "play" button. The gangster opened the door and a thin baby-faced guy stepped nervously into the apartment. The gangster leaned close to the thin guy. "I'll tell you what I'm gonna give you, Snakes," the gangster sneered. "I'm gonna give you to the count of ten to get your ugly, yellow, no-good face off my property before I pump you fulla lead."

"Awright, Johnny. I'm sorry. I'm goin'," the thin guy gasped, backing away.

"One, two . . . ten!" the gangster snarled.

The next thing Kevin knew, the gangster started firing. Kevin's jaw dropped.

"That's not fair!" Kevin shouted at the TV. "He didn't count right!"

On the TV the gangster stopped shooting.

"Keep the change, you filthy animal," he muttered.

Kevin grabbed the remote. He'd seen enough movies to know what was going to happen next. They were going to show the thin guy's bullet-riddled body. He hit the "stop" button just in time, then stood in the middle of the family room, trembling. He looked out the window. It had been gray outside all day, but now it was starting to get dark. All of a sudden he felt very scared and very alone.

Harry and Marv had just finished looting the house next to the McCallisters'. Now they sat in their van, surveying the street. Harry glanced at his wristwatch.

"Check this out," he said. "All these houses have automatic timers to turn on the lights at night even if no one's home. It's time for the Murphys' house to light up."

Across the street the lights in the Murphys' house went on.

"Now doesn't that make you think the Murphys are home?" Marv laughed.

"Here come the McCallisters'," Harry said. Across the street a few lights went on in Kevin's house.

"Looks like Mr. McCallister's trying to save on his electric bill," Marv said.

"Don't kid yourself," Harry said. "That's the one, Marv. That's the silver tuna."

"Oh, yeah?"

"It's loaded," Harry said. "Top-flight goods. Antiques, collectables, objects d'art, VCRs, stereos, TVs. I say we're looking at jewelry, a nice stash of cash, maybe a couple of marketable securities. It's a gem, Marv."

"Then let's rob it," Marv said eagerly.

"Naw, we gotta unload all the stuff we took from the other houses first," said Harry. "We'll come back and hit it later."

December 22
Somewhere Over the Atlantic
5:30 P.M.

Kate was trying to breathe steadily and not go completely berserk. The copilot of the plane, a young man who looked barely old enough to shave, was talking to her.

"I'm sorry, Mrs. McCallister," he said. "But we never turn a plane around. Not even for first-class passengers. Besides, we're closer to Paris now than Chicago."

"But my helpless seven-year-old baby isn't in Paris," Kate snapped angrily. "He's all by himself back in Chicago!"

The copilot said he was sorry again and returned to the cockpit. Kate slumped back in her seat and pressed her fingers over her eyes.

"I don't understand it," said Heather. She and Buzz had come up from the coach seats to find out what was going on. "I *know* I counted eleven kids."

"Listen, everyone," Peter said soothingly. "Kevin's an intelligent boy. He won't do anything stupid."

"He can't even make a sandwich!" Kate cried.

"I read that people can live on water for weeks," said Buzz, trying to be helpful.

"Go away!" Kate screamed at him. The other first-class passengers stared at her, but Kate didn't care. Aunt Leslie put her hand on Kate's shoulder.

"We'll call as soon as we land," she squeaked. "I'm sure everything's okay."

Meanwhile, Uncle Frank took Peter aside.

"Listen," Frank said. "If it'll make you feel any better, I forgot my reading glasses."

Peter stared back at Frank. I can't believe this idiot is my brother, he thought.

DECEMBER 22
OAK PARK
6 P.M.

Harry parked the van in the McCallisters' driveway. Marv reached behind the seat for the crowbar.

"Man, I can taste it," Harry said as he got out. "I'm telling you, Marv, this is the score that's gonna set us up for life."

"How do you want to go in?" Marv asked, tapping the crowbar against his palm.

"Same way as the others," Harry said. "All these houses have stairs in the back leading down to the cellar. We go in and out through the cellar. That way no one sees us from the street."

He and Marv headed for the back of the house.

Kevin sat in the study trying to watch TV. Some lights had gone on before. Kevin knew they were connected to the automatic timer his dad had installed. But his father had only hooked the timer up to a few lights and the house seemed dim and spooky. Well, there was an easy way to fix that. Kevin went upstairs and started turning on all the lights.

Marv had no trouble breaking the lock on the cellar door. He took out a tiny pen flashlight and looked around.

"Wow, what a mess," he whispered to Harry. Parts of mannequins were lying here and there, along with cans of paint and roof tar, boxes of Christmas ornaments, and all kinds of gardening tools.

"We're not here to clean," Harry hissed behind him. "We're here to rob the place. Now come on."

Kevin finished turning on the upstairs lights and started downstairs. He got to the kitchen and turned on the counter TV and the radio, too. Then, for extra good measure, he hit the switch near the door that turned on the basement lights.

In the basement Harry and Marv were suddenly bathed in light.

"What the — ?" Marv gasped.

"We gotta get out of here!" Harry hissed.

They turned and ran as fast as they could without knocking anything over. Moments later they climbed out of the basement, got into the van and pulled out of the driveway.

"Anyone see us?" Harry asked as they sped away down the street.

"I didn't see anyone in the windows," said Marv. "I thought you said they were gone."

"We both watched them leave this morning, birdbrain," Harry snapped.

"Then who was that?" Marv asked.

"I don't know," Harry said. "I didn't see anyone. I swear I don't get it. I *know* they all left."

"And I know I ain't goin' near that house again," Marv said.

"Cool it." Harry ran his fingers over his hair. "I'm gonna figure this thing out and then we are going back. That's the best house on the block."

DECEMBER 23
ORLY AIRPORT, PARIS
1 A.M. (PARIS TIME)

As soon as the plane reached the gate, Kate ran into the terminal and headed for the telephones. The other McCallisters were right behind her.

"I'm going to try our house," Kate yelled. "Peter, you call the Murphys. If they're home they can run over and get Kev. Kids, go get change. Start calling everyone you know."

Kate pulled her address book out of her bag and tossed it to Leslie. "You and Frank call anyone who lives on our street. If we're lucky, someone will still be home."

They took up a whole bank of phones. As Kate dialed her home phone number she felt reassured. *One* of them had to get through.

A moment later she heard a recording that

her phone was out of order. Darn! Kate thought. She had a vague recollection of the man from Commonwealth Power and Light saying something that morning about the phones.

Next Kate tried the local police.

"Oak Park police department," the switchboard operator answered.

Kate waved excitedly at Peter. Then she tried to explain to the operator that she and her family were in Paris, but they'd forgotten Kevin.

"So you want to report a missing child?" the operator asked.

"No," Kate said. "He's not missing. He's at home. We left on an overseas flight and we had eleven kids. Somehow we overlooked him."

"Then the child is not missing," the operator said.

"Listen," Kate said, feeling her frustration growing. "I just need someone to go to my house and see if my child is all right."

"And tell him we're coming home for him," Peter added.

"Right," said Kate. "We're coming home."

"I better connect you with family crisis intervention," said the operator.

"Wait," Kate yelled, "it's not a family crisis!"

But it was too late; the operator put her on hold. Kate turned to Peter.

"Somehow I'm going to make them understand what's going on," she said. "You should go to the ticket counter. Book the first flight home."

"For all of us?" Peter asked.

"There's no sense in taking the kids," Kate said. "You stay here with them. I'll go get Kevin and bring him back."

Peter frowned. Kate gave him a kiss on the cheek. "Just hold Christmas for us, okay?"

Peter nodded and hurried toward the ticket counter. Meanwhile a new voice from the Oak Park police station came on the phone.

"Family crisis intervention. Sergeant Balzak speaking."

"Hi," Kate said. "Look, I'm calling from Paris — "

"Paris?" Sergeant Balzak repeated. "That doesn't sound like it's in our district."

"It isn't," Kate said. "But my little boy is. You see, he's home alone — "

"Has the child been involved in a violent altercation with a drunken or mentally ill family member?" Sergeant Balzak asked.

"No," Kate said. "Let me — "

"Has the child been involved in a household accident?"

"God, I hope not," said Kate. "I — "

"Has the child swallowed poison or an object that has become lodged in his throat?" asked Balzak.

"NO!" Kate screamed. "He's just home alone!

I just want you to send someone over to the house! Just to check on him!"

"Hold your horses, lady," Balzak said. "All you want is someone to go over to your house and check on your son?"

"YES!" screamed Kate.

"Hold on while I transfer you to the police department," Balzak said.

"But I've already — " Before Kate could say anything more, she was put on hold again. She felt like throwing the receiver against the wall, but that wouldn't help get Kevin. Meanwhile the kids, Leslie, and Frank started drifting toward her.

"Any luck?" Kate asked hopefully as she waited for the Oak Park police again.

"None," said Heather. The other kids either shook their heads or shrugged.

"Just a bunch of answering machines," squeaked Aunt Leslie.

"Okay, listen," Kate said, handing the phone to her. "I've got the Oak Park police department on the line. Don't get off until they promise to send someone to the house to check on Kevin. I'm going to see if Peter's had any luck with the planes."

Kate ran to the ticket area. Peter was leaning on the counter, talking to a ticket agent. He didn't look happy.

"Any luck?" Kate asked.

"Tonight's flights to Chicago are all booked,"

Peter said. "With standby lists a mile long."

"Let's try another city," Kate said.

"I already did. Detroit, New York, I tried everything."

"What about a private jet?" Kate asked.

"I checked," Peter said. "None available. The first flight I could get you on leaves Monday night."

"Monday?" Kate gasped. "That's two days from now."

"It's the best I could do."

"But that's not good enough," Kate said.

Peter sighed. "Look, honey, we've done all we can here. The kids are exhausted. We're tired. Let's go to my brother Rob's house. We can call the police again from there."

"No," Kate replied very firmly. "I have a young child at home alone. We punished him last night. He may even be thinking we left him home on purpose. I'm not leaving here unless it's on an airplane."

"Honey, please," Peter begged.

"Don't, Peter," Kate said. "The only place I'm going is back home. I'll put myself on standby for every flight back to the States and just wait until a seat opens up. You take everybody to Rob's. I'll call you as soon as I know anything."

"You sure?" Peter asked.

"Absolutely," said Kate.

Peter smiled slightly. "You're a good mother."

Kate tried to smile back. "I'm trying."

DECEMBER 22
OAK PARK
8:15 P.M.

Kevin wandered into the study. He knew what was about to happen. He was about to spend his first night ever alone. He'd just finished going through the house, making sure the doors were locked and every possible light was on.

"Don't be scared," he whispered. "Dad always says there's nothing to be scared of."

He turned on the TV. A football game was about to begin. The players on the sidelines were walking back and forth pumping their fists, getting themselves up for the game.

Kevin clenched his fists and started walking back and forth. "I won't be afraid," he chanted. "I won't be afraid . . . I'm not afraid. I'm not afraid of anything. Not even the dark."

Kevin stopped and looked at the front door.

He felt really pumped up now. He pushed open the door and went out into the dark.

"I'm not afraid of anyone," he whispered.

"I'm not afraid of *anything*," he said a little louder.

Then he ran down to the end of the driveway and shouted, "I'm not afraid of anyone!"

"That's good," someone said.

Kevin's jaw fell open. Old man Marley came out of the shadows carrying a snow shovel.

"AAAhhhhhhhhhhhh!" Kevin screamed and bolted for the house. He slammed the front door closed, locked it, ran upstairs and dove into his mother's bed. He pulled a pillow over his head and trembled.

Moments later an Oak Park police car rolled down the street. The two officers inside had just received a call from the station to check out the McCallister house and see if anyone was home. Something about the family being in Paris and missing a kid. The cops pulled into the driveway and got out. They went to the door and knocked.

Upstairs, Kevin pulled another pillow over his head and held his breath.

The cop knocked again.

"Go away, Marley," Kevin whispered. *"Please go away!"*

The cops looked in the windows.

"There's nobody home," one of the cops said. "The place looks secure."

"What about the lights?" asked his partner.

"Timers. All the houses around here have 'em."

"So what do we do?" his partner asked.

The first cop shrugged. "Call the station. Tell the McCallisters to count their kids again."

DECEMBER 23
PARIS
3 P.M. (PARIS TIME)

Paris was gaily lit for the holidays. The trees along the Champs Élysées were strung with colored lights and the Arc de Triomphe was bathed in spotlights. But in Rob McCallister's apartment on the Rue de les Fairds, all was not cheery.

Inside, Uncle Frank, Rod, Megan and Linnie sat on the couch and watched TV just like they did at home. Buzz was looking at French magazines and Peter was on the phone to the states, still trying to find someone in Oak Park to check on Kevin.

"Hey, kids," Uncle Frank said. "In honor of our first lunch in France, I'm gonna do a snail burp."

He let out a tiny, high-pitched burp. Megan

groaned and wandered over to Buzz.

"This is so pointless," she complained.

"What?" asked Buzz. He liked these French magazines. Sometimes the models didn't wear a lot of clothes.

"We're sitting here rotting in an apartment," Megan moped. "Kevin's home. Mom's at the airport. . . ."

"So?" Buzz asked.

"You don't think it's weird?" asked Megan.

"No."

"You're not worried about Kevin at all?" Megan asked.

Buzz shrugged. "Why should I?"

"He's home alone," said Megan.

"And he deserves it," said Buzz. "He acted like a jerk once too many times and it finally caught up to him."

"But he's so little and helpless," Megan said. "Think about it. He must be flipping out."

"Yeah," Buzz said with a nasty grin. "He's probably doing a stage-ten brain fry-down right now. But he asked for it."

Megan was shocked. "You're really cruel, you know that?"

"Why?" Buzz asked. "Because I think the little trout can use a couple of days in the real world?"

"You're not at all worried something might happen to him?" Megan asked.

"No." Buzz shook his head and held up three fingers. "For three reasons. A, I'm not that lucky. Two, we have smoke detectors. D, we live on the single most boring street in the United States of America where nothing even remotely dangerous is ever . . . did ever . . . and will ever happen. Period."

Megan knew Buzz was probably right, but she was still worried. She walked over to her father, who'd just hung up the phone. "Any luck?" she asked.

Peter shook his head. "I've spoken to more answering machines in the last four hours than I have in the last four years."

"Is there anyone left to call?" Megan asked.

"Yeah, a few," Peter said. "But I'm gonna try later. Right now all I'm doing is striking out."

DECEMBER 23
OAK PARK
10 A.M.

Kevin walked proudly toward the village of Oak Park. He had just done several very adult things and was quite pleased with himself.

To start with, Kevin had spent the whole night at home alone. He'd even managed to sleep for awhile.

Then this morning, for the first time in his life he'd taken a shower all by himself, and washed every part of his body with actual soap, including all the major crevices . . . like those between his toes, *and* his belly button, which he had never washed before. He was surprised to find that he sort of enjoyed it.

He had also washed his hair with adult-formula shampoo and used a cream rinse for that just-washed shine.

The only thing he hadn't done was brush his teeth, mostly because he couldn't find his toothbrush. But that was why he was doing another incredibly grown-up thing today — he was walking to town, by himself, to buy a toothbrush.

Kevin passed the church and Santa's Village, where Santa sat in a hut and his elf brought in all the kids to see him. He reached into his pocket and felt money he'd taken from the tin box on top of Buzz's shelf. In the process he'd accidentally knocked down a book, which hit Axl's terrarium and broke it. Axl the tarantula had escaped, but Kevin planned to find him later. As for the money, Kevin didn't think Buzz would mind, wherever he was.

The only scary part about going out alone was walking down his street, past all the bushes and hedges. Old man Marley could've been hiding behind any of them. But Kevin had done it and now he was entering the village of Oak Park with its ice-skating pond and quaint two-story brick buildings. And he was no longer worried about old man Marley.

Kevin passed the post office and the butcher and the candy store. It was getting close to lunchtime and he was feeling a little hungry. He knew that with the money in his pocket he could have bought a ton of candy, but he was being grown-up. And that meant buying a toothbrush instead.

If I keep this up, Kevin thought, I'll almost qualify to be a teenager.

Ding-a-ling! A little bell rang as Kevin stepped into the drugstore. He wandered past shelves filled with shampoo and deodorants and Dr. Scholl's foot stuff until he found the toothbrush rack. Kevin had never realized how many different sizes, shapes and colors of toothbrushes there were. He could only assume that people must've brushed their teeth a lot. Maybe even once a week.

Kevin picked a red brush with white-and-blue bristles and took it to the counter. An old lady with a painted face stared down at him. She was a little scary-looking, but he could deal with her.

"How may I help you?" she asked.

"Is this toothbrush approved by the American Dental Association?" Kevin asked. The old lady held the toothbrush close to her face and tried to read the tiny print on the side of the package.

Ding-a-ling! Someone else entered the drugstore, but neither Kevin nor the old lady bothered to look. They were too busy trying to figure out whether the toothbrush was approved or not.

"It doesn't say, hon," the old lady said, putting the toothbrush down on the counter. "Let me ask my husband."

She walked toward the back where the prescriptions were filled. "Herb, I have a question about a toothbrush," she said.

Kevin picked up the toothbrush and stared at

the label, but there were too many big words. All of a sudden out of the corner of his eye he noticed someone coming down the aisle toward him. There was something disturbingly familiar about that slow limping shuffle.

A large bloody hand slapped down on the counter. Kevin's heart started to race as his eyes followed the long tattered sleeve of the overcoat up to . . .

Old man Marley!

Kevin backed away. Old man Marley waved the bloody hand at him.

"Cut it on my snow shovel," he said. "On the sharp edge."

Kevin took another step back. His mouth was dry, and goose bumps raced up and down his arms. His heart beat like a drum. Meanwhile the old lady came back to the counter.

"Hon, I'm sorry, we don't know if — "

Kevin didn't hear her. He was backing toward the door.

"Hon?" the old lady said. "You pay for that here."

Kevin was staring at Marley's bloody hand and thinking about the snow shovel with the sharp edge. Sharp enough to kill people. Even a whole family!

"Little boy!" the old lady called. "Come back and pay for that please."

Kevin couldn't believe he made it to the door alive. He pushed it open and ran outside.

A moment later the old lady reached the door. "Hey, stop that boy!" she shouted. "Darn, these shoplifters get younger all the time!"

Shoplifter? Kevin stopped on the sidewalk and turned. But he wasn't a . . .

A police car came around the corner. The old lady was pointing at Kevin. The police car stopped and a cop got out.

"See that boy?" the old lady shouted. "He just robbed my store!"

Kevin's eyes went wide. That was a lie! Why was she saying that? But the police officer was coming toward him and he was big and scary. Kevin turned and ran as fast as he could down the sidewalk. Ahead people were skating on the pond. Kevin raced toward them and dove stomach first, like Pete Rose. Skaters jumped out of the way as he shot across the ice.

Behind him the policeman hit the ice and flipped backward. Then two skaters fell on top of him.

Kevin reached the other side of the pond and raced down the street. He passed Santa's Village and the church and had to run around the life-sized nativity scene of Joseph and Mary and the little drummer boy standing over the manger. He turned down Rivard Street and headed toward his house, cutting through backyards.

Finally he jumped over a fence into his own backyard. He quickly pulled open the kitchen door, then slammed it behind him and leaned against it, trembling. As he slowly calmed down he became aware of something in his clenched hand. Kevin looked down. *The toothbrush!* He felt a new wave of fright wash over him. He really was in trouble. Not only had he made his family disappear, but now the police would be after him.

"I'm a criminal," he whispered.

Meanwhile, in the Bensons' house next to old man Marley's place, two real criminals were hard at work taking what wasn't theirs.

"I'm telling you," Harry said as he dumped out the Bensons' dresser drawers on the bedroom floor. "There's something screwy about that McCallister house."

"But we saw the lights go on," Marv said. "*After* the timer lights."

"Yeah, but here's what I figure," Harry said. "These people know us burglars know about those timers. So if this guy McCallister is smart, he gets *two* timers. So the first one turns on a few lights and we think it's the timer. But when the second set of lights go on we're supposed to think it's real people."

"That's pretty advanced thinking," Marv said. "I say we just forget the McCallister place."

"I'm tellin' you, Marv, that house is ripe," said Harry.

Just then the phone rang and the Bensons' answering machine clicked on. Both crooks stared at it.

"Hello, you have reached the home of Bill, Betsy, Bonnie, and Barry Benson, but we're not here. Please leave your name and phone number after the beep and we'll get back to you as soon as possible."

The caller started to speak. "Hi, it's Peter McCallister again. We're at my brother's apartment in Paris. The number here is — "

Marv stepped over and turned off the speaker. He smiled at Harry. "Okay, you're right. They're in Paris. The guy's just got two timers going. When do you want to hit the place?"

"Suppose we finish up this side of the street first," Harry said. "Then we'll do it. Like I always say, save the best for last."

December 23
Orly Airport
8:30 p.m. (Paris Time)

Kate had put herself on standby for no less than fifteen flights back to the States and hadn't come close to getting on any of them. She couldn't stop thinking of Kevin, alone, frightened, helpless in that house. What a terrifying experience for a seven-year-old. It was probably doing irreversible psychological damage to him. She imagined coming home and finding him curled up in a corner sucking his thumb.

Kate was starting to feel desperate. And that meant taking desperate action. A flight to Chicago was scheduled to leave in half an hour. The waiting list was so long the airline wouldn't even let her put her name on it. But there were other ways to get on board.

Kate spotted a plump middle-aged woman

carrying a heavy handbag and wearing a Chicago Cubs baseball cap. The woman was headed for the Chicago departure gate . . . until Kate stepped in her way.

"Excuse me," Kate said. "I must get on that flight to Chicago, but there's no room. So here's my offer. I have five hundred dollars, a pocket translator, and two first-class tickets for a flight leaving next week. I'll trade it all for your coach ticket."

The woman stopped and thought. She was looking at Kate's wristwatch.

"Is that a real Rolex?" the woman asked.

"Yes." Kate held up the watch. "See how the second hand sweeps instead of ticking to each second? That's how you can tell."

The woman nodded. "What else you got?"

"Well." Kate thought fast and then started pulling her jewelry off. "I've got this gold necklace, bracelet, and sapphire ring."

"That is a nice ring," the woman said. Kate felt encouraged. The woman actually seemed interested. Then a portly man wearing a hearing aid and a Chicago White Sox cap came by.

"Come on, Irene," the man said. "They're gonna board soon."

"Wait, Ed," Irene said. "This woman's offering us two first-class tickets to Chicago for next week, plus a ring, a pocket translator, five hundred dollars, and — "

"I'll throw in the Samsonite luggage," Kate offered eagerly.

Ed took off his cap and scratched his head. "It's a nice offer, but what about our Christmas plans?"

"Don't forget the bracelet," Kate said.

"I didn't care for the bracelet," said Irene. Kate showed it to Ed in case he liked it. She was so close! She couldn't let them slip through her fingers now.

"Naw, I don't like the bracelet, either," Ed said. He started to pull Irene away. "Thanks, anyway."

"But the ring!" Kate said, following them. "You liked the ring, ma'am."

"She's got plenty of rings," Ed said, pulling his wife harder. "Now come on, Irene. Let's go!"

"Wait!" Kate begged. "Please . . . my little boy's home all by himself. I'm desperate. I beg you. From a mother to a mother. *Please?"*

"Ed?" Irene was wavering. She looked back at her husband.

Ed tapped his ear. "Say what? Darn hearing aid went out. Come on, honey." He yanked her away.

Kate stood in the middle of the gate area as passengers rushed past her to board the plane. She was almost ready to cry. Was there no humanity left in this world?

December 23
Oak Park
3:30 P.M.

Kevin stayed in the house. He was terrified that the police or old man Marley would get him. But there was nothing left to eat that was easily nukable or could be consumed straight from the box. And he was getting hungry.

With about an hour of sunlight left, Kevin made a bold decision. There was a grocery store down the street from Santa's Village. If he wore a red ski hat pulled low, a passing policemen might not recognize him. As far as old man Marley was concerned, Kevin would have to take his chances.

Kevin left his house and ran across the street. Once he was past old man Marley's house, he started to walk backward, to make sure the old man didn't sneak up on him from behind like he had in the drugstore.

What Kevin didn't know was that Harry and Marv had just finished ransacking the Bensons' house and were quietly backing their van down the driveway. Kevin continued to walk backward. It was just luck that Harry saw him in the rearview mirror and jammed on the brakes.

The sound of the van skidding made Kevin jump and turn around. The van slid to a halt right in front of him. Kevin looked up as Harry rolled down the driver's window.

"Gotta keep an eye out for traffic, son," Harry said.

"Yeah," Marv added. "Santa don't visit funeral homes."

Kevin just stared up at Harry. *That gold tooth!*

"Step back, kid," Harry said and backed the van into the street. Kevin stood on the sidewalk and watched. It was the policeman who'd come over the other night! Only now he was disguised as a plumber. Kevin quickly figured out that the police were wearing disguises so they could sneak up and get him for stealing the toothbrush. And he'd used it already so he couldn't even give it back!

Harry knew the kid was watching him. He stopped the van in the middle of the street. Kevin started to walk away. He knew it was wrong to take the toothbrush, but it had been an accident. And no one should go to jail because of an accident.

Harry frowned as he watched Kevin.

"What's the matter?" Marv asked.

"That kid looked at me funny," Harry said.

"You ever seen him before?"

"I don't know," Harry said. "I saw a lot of kids this week."

"Watch which house he goes to," Marv said.

Kevin got to the sidewalk on the other side of the street. He peeked over his shoulder. The undercover cops in the van were still watching him. Kevin was so scared he wanted to cry. His house was right in front of him and he wanted to run inside, but then the cops would know where he lived. He took a deep breath and started to walk toward the corner.

The van started to follow. Kevin glanced behind and started to run. The van picked up speed. Kevin ducked around the corner and onto the church property.

The van turned the corner next to the church and screeched to a stop. Harry and Marv jumped out and looked around. But the street was empty and the church doors were locked. The kid wasn't hiding behind any shrubs.

"How could he disappear like that?" Harry asked.

"Let's forget it, okay?" Marv said. "We shouldn't be chasing a kid anyway. It's like sending an invitation to the cops."

"I just don't like the way he looked at me," Harry said.

"Don't sweat it," Marv said. "Look, we're doin' great. We'll drop off the Bensons' stuff and come back later for the McCallister house. If no one's home we're in fat city."

The two crooks got back into the van and drove away. Hidden in the nativity scene, Kevin waited until the van's taillights disappeared. Then he took off the drummer boy's robe and put down the drum — he had overheard every word the two crooks had said. Kevin started to run home. It was getting dark and he was too scared to go to the grocery store anyway.

Those guys weren't policemen after all. They were robbers! They'd just robbed the Bensons' house and were planning to rob his house next!

He let himself back into his house. He wanted to cry. Why had he been so mean to his family? Why did he have to wish that they'd disappear? His stomach growled. Kevin looked around and clenched his fist. He'd have to figure out some other way of feeding himself tonight. And he'd also have to figure out how to keep those robbers away. It was too bad he was wanted by the police, because he could sure use some help. Now he'd have to do it alone.

He locked the front door and secured it with the chain.

"This is my house," he whispered. "And I have to defend it."

December 23
Oak Park
7 p.m.

To protect his home, Kevin enlisted the help of the mannequins from the basement, a "laugh box" that belonged to Jeff and the piano in the living room. From the empty pizza boxes in the kitchen he got the phone number of Little Nero's Pizza.

"I'd like one plain pizza," he told the man on the phone.

"Anything to drink?" the man asked.

"A Pepsi, please," Kevin said. "Uh, on second thought, make it a six-pack."

"One plain pizza, one six-pack Pepsi," the man said. "Be about twenty minutes."

Kevin knew the key to defending his house was not to let anyone know he was home alone. And that included the pizza delivery boy. He had an idea and ran into the study.

Kevin had just finished connecting the VCR to the TV on the kitchen counter when he heard the pizza delivery car pull up outside. He stood in the foyer and listened as the delivery boy went up the front walk and then stopped on the porch to read the note Kevin had left directing him to the kitchen door behind the house. Kevin raced into the kitchen and set the tape in the VCR to the right place in the gangster movie. A moment later the pizza boy knocked. Kevin pushed "play" and turned up the volume on the VCR.

"Who is it?" the scar-faced gangster in the movie asked. Kevin hit "pause."

"Little Nero's Pizza, sir!" the delivery boy outside said.

It's working! Kevin thought as he fast forwarded the tape to the next scene and pushed "play."

"Leave it on the doorstep and get outa here," the gangster snapped on the VCR.

"But what about the money?" the pizza delivery boy asked.

Kevin raced to the next place on the tape.

"What money?" the gangster asked.

"Well, you have to pay for the pizza," the boy said timidly. A second later Kevin hit "play" again.

"Is that a fact?" the gangster snarled. "How much do I owe you?"

"With the Pepsi it comes to fourteen dollars and eighty cents," the boy said.

Kevin carefully pulled the money out of his pocket and pushed it through Ralphy's doggie door. Then he fast forwarded and hit the "play" button again.

"Keep the change, you filthy animal," the gangster snarled.

Outside the delivery boy picked up the bills. The change came to twenty cents. Cheapskate, he thought.

Kevin let the tape run. He turned on a desk lamp he'd brought down from Buzz's room and then stood in front of it with the BB gun. The shadow he cast against the kitchen curtains made him look bigger than Captain America.

Outside, the delivery boy saw the shadow. The gun barrel poked out ominously. On the VCR the gangster said, "I'm gonna give you to the count of ten to get your ugly, yellow, no-good face off my property!"

The delivery boy started backing away. Sometimes this job just wasn't worth the hassles.

"One, two! . . . ten!" the gangster shouted.

The delivery boy turned and ran.

Kevin stood in the foyer and listened to the sound of the delivery car's tires peeling out of the driveway.

"It worked!" he whispered. "I actually scared someone bigger than me away!"

He went back to the kitchen door and got the pizza and Pepsi. Now for the reward!

* * *

Kevin had just finished his second slice of pizza when he heard the van pull into the driveway. He jumped up and raced into the living room.

Outside Harry and Marv quietly got out of the van. The lights were on in the McCallister house and the drapes were closed.

"Okay, Marv," Harry said. "Get the crowbar and let's go to work."

Marv had just come back from the van when they both heard something that made them stop.

"What's that?" Marv gasped.

"I don't know," Harry said. "Sounds like piano music."

"Like a kid playing or something," Marv said. The two crooks scowled at each other.

"We gotta check this out," Harry said.

They crept through the shadows around to the side of the house. Suddenly Harry froze.

"Look at that!" he whispered. In the window they could see the shadows of two people sitting in chairs, nodding their heads to a very poor rendition of "Joy to the World" on the piano. Every time the piano player hit a wrong key, the two people laughed.

"I don't get it," Marv whispered. "Did they come home?"

"From Paris?" Harry wondered.

Inside Kevin nervously picked through "Joy to the World" for the third time. Near him two of his mother's mannequins sat in chairs. One was dressed in Peter's clothes, the other in Kate's. A string attached to their heads ran down to the floor and across to Kevin's ankle. By moving his foot slightly, Kevin made the mannequins' heads nod. Every time Kevin made a mistake on the piano, he reached down to the bench and pressed the button on Jeff's laugh box.

Outside, the two crooks couldn't figure it out.

"That was the fastest trip to Paris I ever heard of," Marv said.

"I dunno," Harry said. "It still don't make sense."

"Well, somebody's in there now," Marv said. "We gotta split before they see us."

"Yeah," Harry said, slowly backing away. "We'll come back tomorrow. Maybe they'll be gone by then."

Kevin was incredibly relieved when he heard the van pull out of the driveway. Once again he'd successfully fooled them. He was getting good at this.

December 23
Oak Park
9 P.M.

Kevin lay on his mother's bed. His mind was racing. He'd had more excitement in one day than he'd probably had in his whole life. But now he was tired and lonely. On the nightstand was a family portrait in a silver frame. Kevin picked it up. There was his mom and dad, Buzz, Megan, Linnie, and Jeff. Kevin felt his eyes start to grow watery.

"Listen, you guys," he whispered. "I didn't mean to make you disappear. Honest. If you come back I'll never be a pain again. I promise."

He kissed the picture and put it back on the nightstand. Then he went to sleep. With the lights on.

DECEMBER 24: CHRISTMAS EVE PARIS 5 A.M. (PARIS TIME)

In the gray of dawn at Orly Airport Kate slept across three seats in the passenger lounge, using her purse for a pillow. Overhead a loudspeaker crackled to life:

"This is the final boarding call for American Airlines flight five-six-one to Boston, connecting to Detroit. Will standby passenger McCallister please come to the ticket counter."

Kate rose, almost in a trance, and propelled herself toward the counter. Finally . . . she was going home . . . to her baby.

A few miles away, in her uncle Rob's apartment, Linnie McCallister lay awake in bed, watching the sky grow slowly brighter as a new day began. A new day without Kevin. Somewhere in the house a phone rang. Next to Linnie, Megan stirred and rolled over. The two sisters stared at each other.

"How come you're up?" Megan asked.

"The same reason you are," Linnie said. "I'm worried about Kevin."

"Yeah," Megan admitted. "Hard to believe."

"He may be a pain," Linnie said, "but look at it from his point of view. We do dump on him a lot."

"I guess," Megan said. "All I know is I'd feel a lot better if he was here or we were there."

Linnie nodded and got out of bed.

"Where're you going?" Megan asked.

"To get some orange juice," Linnie said.

She stepped out into the hall. On the way to the kitchen she passed the room Jeff and Buzz were sharing. Linnie peeked in. Jeff was lying in bed, staring at the ceiling. Buzz was snoring like a bear. Linnie went into the kitchen. She was surprised to find her father, in his robe, staring out the window.

"Dad?"

Peter turned around. "What're you doing up, sweetheart?"

"Couldn't sleep," Linnie said with a shrug. "Heard anything from Mom?"

"She just called from the airport," Peter said. "She caught a flight to Detroit. She'll be with Kevin by tonight."

"Which means she won't be here for Christmas," Linnie said. "And neither will Kevin. It won't even be like Christmas."

"We'll just delay it a little bit," Peter said to reassure her.

"I think it's a bad idea," Linnie said.

"But we don't have any choice, sweetheart," Peter said.

"All I know is families shouldn't be apart on Christmas, no matter how mean they are to each other the rest of the year," Linnie said. "It's not right, Daddy. Us here, them there. Christmas isn't about being in Paris. It's about being together."

Peter looked up at his daughter in awe. She was right. How come a twelve-year-old understood these things better than he did?

December 24
Oak Park
10 A.M.

Kevin had a plan for getting his family back. That was why he was pushing a cart through the grocery store. To avoid detection he wore one of Buzz's baseball caps low on his head and the collar of his coat pulled high.

He picked up a half-gallon of milk and moved on to the bread section, where he squeezed several loaves for freshness.

"Pushing the cart for mommy?" someone said.

Kevin turned around and looked up at a middle-aged woman with streaked blonde hair. "Yes, ma'am."

"What a good little helper you are," the woman said. "I'll bet you get lots of swell things from Santa tomorrow morning."

"You never know," Kevin said. There was only

one thing he wanted for Christmas. His family back. The woman started to push her cart away, but Kevin needed some help.

"Excuse me," he said. "Could you tell me what the stuff is that you put in the washing machine to make clothes feel as fluffy soft as a kitten and smell as fresh as a springtime breeze?"

The woman frowned, then smiled. "Oh, you mean fabric softener. It's two aisles over."

"Thank you," Kevin said. "And have a merry Christmas."

When Kevin had everything he needed, he pushed his cart up to the checkout counter. A bored-looking older girl was behind the cash register. She looked about Heather's age.

"Hi," said Kevin. The girl ignored him and started ringing up his stuff. First the milk, then fabric softener, bread, soup, and a microwave macaroni-and-cheese dinner. Kevin picked up a *Woman's Day* magazine and thumbed through it. He found a recipe for Macafurters.

"I wish I could use the stove," he said, holding up the magazine for the girl to see. "I'd make some of these Macafurters. They look good, don't they?"

The girl nodded and rang up a large package of plastic Army men.

"Uh, for the kids," Kevin said.

The last item was a half-gallon of orange juice.

"Hold it," Kevin said, handing her a coupon. "It was in the paper this morning."

The girl rang up juice minus the coupon. "That'll be nineteen dollars and eighty-three cents."

Kevin gave her a twenty-dollar bill. "Keep the change," he said.

DECEMBER 24
OAK PARK
2 P.M.

The van was parked all the way at the end of the Murphys' driveway. From there Harry and Marv could see into the McCallisters' backyard.

"Looks awful quiet," Harry said.

"Maybe they're still asleep," said Marv.

"At two in the afternoon?" Harry asked. "No way. Something ain't right. Last night the place was jumpin'. Now it don't seem like anybody's home. I can't figure it."

He pushed open the van door.

"What're you doing?" Marv asked.

"Wait here," Harry said.

Inside the house, Kevin was standing at the kitchen sink, doing the dishes. If he was going to get what he wanted for Christmas, he was going to have to be extra, extra good. That's why he went down to the basement before and did all the family laundry. Now he was cleaning the rest of the house.

Kevin looked outside at the bare brown lawn. He was trying to save all his wish power to bring his family back and didn't want to waste any on a white Christmas. But it sure would be —

Suddenly Kevin froze. A dish slipped out of his hands and back into the soapy water. To his horror, the guy from the van, the phony policeman, began to emerge from the bushes. Kevin quickly pulled the kitchen curtains closed. He whipped off his rubber gloves and flicked on the VCR.

Harry stepped softly across the back porch to the kitchen door. He tried to peek in through the curtains. Then he pushed open the doggie door with his foot.

Inside Kevin held his breath as the doggie door flapped open. His heart started to pound as the kitchen doorknob rattled. He pushed the "play" button on the VCR and the gangster movie went on.

"All right, Johnny," the thin kid said. "But what about my money?"

"What money?" snapped the gangster.

The sudden sound of voices from inside made Harry jump back.

"Acey said you'd have some dough for me."

Acey? Harry scowled. He stepped up to the kitchen door and pressed his ear against it.

"Is that a fact?" the gangster said. "How much do I owe you?" While the gangster movie continued to play on the VCR, Kevin carefully opened a pack of Buzz's firecrackers.

"I'll tell you what I'm gonna give you, Snakes," the gangster said.

Snakes? Harry thought.

"I'm gonna give you to the count of ten to get your ugly, yellow, no-good face off my property before I pump you fulla lead," the gangster snarled.

Harry's eyes went wide. Inside a frightened voice was saying, "Awright, Johnny. I'm sorry. I'm goin'."

Kevin lit a match and held the firecrackers over a wastebasket. The gangster was counting.

"One, two! . . . ten!"

Kevin lit the pack. The fuse sparked and hissed as the firecrackers fell into the wastebasket.

Bang! Bang! Bang! Bang!

Harry dove off the back porch and ran across the yard. He jumped into the van and slammed the door. He was panting.

"What happened?" Marv asked, alarmed.

"Someone just got blown away in there," Harry gasped.

"What!?"

"Someone beat us to the job," Harry said.

"They were in there arguing. Then one blew the other away."

"Do we know 'em?" Marv asked.

"I don't know," Harry said. "Two guys named Snakes and Acey. I thought I recognized one of the voices."

"Snakes?" Marv frowned. "I don't know no Snakes."

"Well, I say we split," Harry said. He started to turn the key in the ignition, but Marv stopped him.

"Wait a minute," he said. "We better see who it is. We're workin' this neighborhood, too. Suppose we get nailed and the cops try to pin this murder on us. It would help if we could steer 'em to the guilty party."

"Good thinking," Harry said, taking the key out of the ignition.

Kevin didn't hear the van leave, but he waited a long time until he was sure it had. Those guys might be grown-ups, but they were pretty easy to fool.

His thoughts turned back to preparations for Christmas. If Santa was going to bring his family back, he had to have a tree. There was no way he could buy one, but maybe there was one in the backyard he could use.

In the van, Marv was asleep. Harry was just starting to doze when the kid came out of the house with a saw. He quickly shook Marv's shoulder.

"It's him!" Harry said. "The kid who looked at me funny. Come on."

Harry and Marv slipped out of the van and cut across the Murphys' yard. They hid behind some bushes and watched Kevin cut the top off a short fir tree and carry it back into the house. Then Harry and Marv snuck up to the living room window.

Inside Kevin put the little tree in the tree stand and started to decorate it. He also put out a glass of milk and a plate of cookies for Santa and some carrots for the reindeer. As he put the carrots under the tree, he happened to glance at the window. His heart almost stopped. One of the bad guys was staring through the glass at him!

"Dad!" Kevin quickly shouted as loud as he could. "Can you come here and help me!?"

Outside the window, Marv quickly pulled Harry back. "Come on! If the kid's there, the parents gotta be!"

"No." Harry shook his head. "He's home . . . alone. I'm telling you, Marv. We've been scammed by a kid."

Inside Kevin raced upstairs and got the BB gun. He stopped on the upstairs landing and listened. There was no sound of breaking glass or anyone forcing their way in. Kevin went into Megan's room and looked through the window.

The bad guys were standing in the backyard right below him. They were talking. Kevin quietly slid open the window and listened.

"You can't be serious," Marv was saying. "You want to come back tonight?"

"You got it," said Harry.

"Even with the kid here?"

"Yup."

"I don't think that's a real bright idea," Marv said.

"Look," Harry said intensely. "What have I been telling you since we started working this block? This house is the one, the silver tuna. I've wanted it ever since I laid eyes on it. To me this house is the difference between a good Christmas and a bad Christmas. And I ain't had a good Christmas in twenty years."

"That long?" Marv was shocked.

"That long," said Harry.

"Well, I don't want to spoil Christmas for ya," Marv said.

"Good," Harry said. "So here's what we do. We take off now for awhile, then come back tonight . . . when it's dark. Say around nine o'clock."

"Yeah," Marv said with a smile. "Kids are scared of the dark."

Upstairs in the house, Kevin slowly slid the window closed. What was he going to do? How would he stop them?

"Mom?" he whispered in a trembling voice. "Where are you?"

DECEMBER 24
LOGAN INTERNATIONAL AIRPORT
BOSTON
4:30 P.M.

Kate stood in the aisle of the 747 from Paris. The plane was at the gate. The layover seemed to be taking forever. A stewardess came by and Kate stopped her.

"Shouldn't we be leaving soon?" Kate asked.

"There's a snowstorm over the eastern Great Lakes," the stewardess said. "We just heard that they may have to shut down Detroit Airport."

"What would that mean?" Kate asked.

"That you'd be having Christmas in Boston," the stewardess replied, and moved on.

Kate moved back to her seat and wearily pressed her forehead against the seat in front of her. She'd been living on catnaps for nearly three days.

"Please," she whispered. "I didn't come this far to be stopped now. *Please!*"

And then, as if someone had heard her, the plane jolted backward from the gate and headed for the runway.

December 24
Oak Park
5 P.M.

Kevin hurried toward Santa's Village. He'd been so involved in preparing for the "visit" he expected from the robbers that he'd forgotten what time it was. Now he was afraid he'd miss Santa altogether.

Ahead he saw a woman in an elf's suit locking the door to Santa's hut.

"Excuse me," Kevin said hastily. "Is he gone?"

"Santa?" the elf said. "Yeah. We're all done here. Elves gotta celebrate Christmas, too."

"But it's really important that I speak to him," Kevin said.

"Well . . ." the elf sighed. "He's around back getting into his car. If you hurry you can catch him."

Kevin ran around the back of the hut in time to see Santa pull a parking ticket off the windshield of a beat-up old car.

"How do you like that?" Santa grumbled. "It's Christmas Eve and Santa gets a parking ticket. What's next? Rabies shots for the Easter bunny?"

"Excuse me," Kevin said. "Can I talk to you for a minute?"

"If you make it quick," Santa said. "Just because I'm Santa Claus doesn't mean I don't celebrate Christmas, too."

"Okay, look," Kevin said, "I know you're not the real Santa Claus. . . ."

"What makes you say that?" Santa asked. "I mean, just out of curiosity?"

"I'm old enough to know how it works," Kevin said.

"Oh, yeah?" said Santa.

"Yeah. I know you only work for him," Kevin said. "But do you think you could get him a message?"

"Sure." Santa smiled.

"I'm Kevin McCallister and I live over on Rivard Street. Now this is really important. Would you please tell Santa that instead of presents this year I just want my family back?"

Santa frowned. "I'm not sure I understand."

"Don't worry," Kevin said. "He'll know. Tell him no toys. Just Peter, Kate, Buzz, Megan, Linnie and Jeff and my cousins and Aunt Leslie . . . and I guess if he has room, Uncle Frank, too. Okay?"

"I'll see what I can do," Santa said.

"I really appreciate it," Kevin said, starting to back away. "Sorry to take up your time."

"Hey, hold on," Santa said, reaching into his pocket. "My elf took the last of the candy canes for her stepkids."

"That's okay," Kevin said.

"Don't be silly," said Santa. "Everyone who sees Santa has to get . . . something."

Santa pulled out a Tic Tac box and shook out two tiny white mints. "Merry Christmas, son. Don't spoil your appetite."

"Merry Christmas to you, too," Kevin said.

Kevin started to walk home. The houses on the street near Santa's Village weren't as big or fancy as the houses in his neighborhood, and it seemed like more of them had real live people inside instead of mannequins. Kevin looked in at the families sitting around their tables eating dinner. They looked happy. Outside on the sidewalk Kevin felt like he was the only kid left on earth.

He turned the corner and started to pass the church. It was all lit up and he could hear a choir singing inside. Kevin knew he had a little time before the crooks came back. He cut across the lawn and pulled open the church doors.

The church was lit with candles and filled with

people. Up front a choir of kids was singing and a man was playing the big organ. Kevin pulled off his hat and pressed it tight against his belly. Some people were standing along the back wall of the church and Kevin stood next to them. For a while he just listened to the music.

"Beautiful, isn't it?" the man next to Kevin said between songs.

"Yeah," Kevin said. "For a bunch of kids, they sing really well."

"Yes, they do," the man smiled.

Kevin looked up. His eyes went wide and he bit his lip in terror. It was old man Marley!

"See that little red-haired girl up there?" Marley pointed toward the choir. Kevin wanted to run, but he also wanted to see what Marley was pointing at.

"She's my granddaughter," Marley said. "About the same age as you. You know her?"

Kevin shook his head slowly. Old man Marley seemed awful friendly for a snow-shovel murderer.

"I know you," Marley said. "Live across the street from me, right?"

Kevin nodded. He was still trembling a little.

"You don't have to be so scared," Marley chuckled. "All that stuff you hear about me . . . none of it's true. Just the product of someone's overactive imagination. . . . So, have you been a good boy this year?"

"I . . . I think so," Kevin stammered.

Marley gave him a look. "You just *think* so?"
Kevin had to shake his head.

"I had a feeling," Marley said. "This is the place to be when you're feeling bad about yourself."

"It is?" Kevin had never thought of church that way. "Are you feeling bad about yourself?"

Marley looked surprised. "No, I came to hear my granddaughter sing."

They both paused to listen to the choir.

"The truth is, I've been kind of a pain lately," Kevin admitted. "I said things I shouldn't have said and did some stuff, too. It's bothering me because I really like my family even though sometimes I say I don't . . . and sometimes I even think I don't. Do you know what I mean?"

"Yup," said Marley. "How you feel about your family is a complicated thing."

"Especially when you have four older brothers and sisters," Kevin said.

"Deep down you always love them," Marley said. "But sometimes you forget and then you hurt them and they hurt you."

"Maybe it's because I'm a kid," Kevin said.

"Oh, no, I don't think so," said Marley. "Actually, it's the reason I'm here right now, too."

"It is?" Kevin was surprised.

"I have to see my granddaughter here because I can't go to her house," Marley said.

"Why not?" Kevin asked.

"A few years back I had an argument with my

son," Marley said. "He's a grown-up, mind you, but just the same we both lost our tempers and said we never wanted to see each other again . . . . Unfortunately, we've both stuck to it."

"Why don't you call him?" Kevin asked.

"Well, I think about it," Marley said, "but I'm afraid he won't talk to me."

Kevin stared up at his old wrinkled face. "Aren't you too old to be afraid?"

"You can never be too old to be afraid, son," Marley said.

Kevin thought for a moment. "I was always afraid of our basement," Kevin said. "It's dark and there's weird stuff down there and it smells funny. But I made myself go down and do some laundry. If you turn on the lights, it's no big deal."

Marley squinted at him. "Are you trying to tell me something?"

"Maybe you should call your son," Kevin said.

"What if he won't talk to me?" Marley asked.

"At least you'll know and you won't have to be afraid anymore," Kevin said.

"I don't know," Marley said, but it seemed to Kevin he was considering it.

"Maybe you should do it for your granddaughter," Kevin said. "I bet she misses you."

"I sure miss her," Marley sighed. Then he put his hand on Kevin's shoulder. Kevin thought it would feel terrible, but it felt good. "You know, son, it's been nice talking to you."

"It's been nice talking to you, too," Kevin said. Suddenly he remembered the crooks.

"Well, merry Christmas," Kevin said.

"Merry Christmas to you," said Marley.

Kevin turned and hurried out of the church. He had a house to defend.

DECEMBER 24
DETROIT METROPOLITAN AIRPORT
8 P.M.

"I'm sorry, Mrs. McCallister," the ticket agent in Detroit was saying, "but you can see for yourself. The weather's horrible. Every flight to Chicago is cancelled."

Kate stared out the plate glass windows of the terminal. It was snowing so hard she could barely see the planes. A few minutes earlier she had staggered off the much-delayed 747 and went straight to the counter and begged the agent to find her a flight to Chicago. She was practically ready to send herself by Federal Express.

"I'll get you a hotel room for the night," the agent said. "I'm sure there'll be an opening on a flight tomorrow afternoon."

"I can't wait that long," Kate said.

"I'm terribly sorry," the ticket agent said. "But I've done everything I can."

Kate reached across the counter and grabbed the startled ticket agent by the lapels.

"Listen to me," she yelled. "I haven't slept more than six hours in the last three days. I've gone from Chicago to Paris to Boston to Detroit, just to get home to my child. And now I'm only a few hundred miles away and you're telling me it's hopeless?"

"It's the weather . . ." The ticket agent's eyes were darting around as he looked for help. Kate pulled him closer.

"It's Christmas," Kate told him. "The season of perpetual hope. I don't care if I have to fly through a three-hundred-mile wall of solid snow. . . . I don't care if it costs me everything I own, or if I have to sell my soul to the devil himself. . . . *I am going home to my son!*"

A hand tapped Kate on the shoulder. She turned, expecting airport security, but instead she found herself facing a curly-haired man wearing blue polyester pants and a red satin jacket with the words "Gus Polinski and the Kenosha Kickers" stitched over the pocket. Kate noticed he was carrying an accordian case.

"Maybe I can help, lady," Gus said.

"Thanks," Kate said, "but I really don't see how — "

"Me and the band" — Gus pointed to half a dozen men also wearing red satin jackets and carrying instrument cases of various sizes and shapes — "just got in from a big polka festival out in Asbury Park, New Jersey. We got a Christmas gig lined up tomorrow in Milwaukee, but our flight's been cancelled so we're gonna drive. Rental car place said we got the last car left in Detroit so I figured since Chicago's on the way, maybe you'd like a lift?"

"Would I ever!?" Kate gasped.

"I just gotta warn you," Gus said. "This storm's headed for Chicago and the roads out there are real bad. It's gonna be a slow trip and we'll be squeezed in tight. All they had was a station wagon. And besides the boys and me, we got a tuba and a bass fiddle."

"Then strap me to the roof," Kate said.

December 24
Oak Park
9 P.M.

Kevin took a steaming container out of the microwave and put it on a place mat on the kitchen table. He'd set the table nicely, just like his mother would have. He sat down and said grace.

"Bless this highly nutritious microwaveable macaroni-and-cheese dinner and the people who sold it on sale. Amen."

He was just about to start eating when a church bell chimed in the distance. Kevin spun around and looked at the kitchen clock. Was it 9 P.M. already? His stomach knotted and his appetite disappeared.

Kevin jumped up and quickly cleared off the kitchen table. Then he grabbed the BB gun. He crouched behind the kitchen curtains and felt his heart pounding.

"This is it," he whispered. "Don't get scared now."

A moment later the van pulled into the driveway and Harry and Marv got out. Harry had the crowbar. In the distance the church bell chimed again.

"How do you want to go in?" Marv asked.

"May as well knock and see if he'll open up," Harry said. He started toward the kitchen door.

"Yeah," said Marv. "He's a kid. Kids are stupid. I know I was."

"You still are," said Harry.

"Maybe, but I was a lot worse," Marv said.

Kevin peeked though the kitchen curtains. When he saw the crooks coming, he backed away and gripped the BB gun tightly. A second later there was a knock on the kitchen door.

"Merry Christmas, little fella," Harry called from outside. "We know you're in there and all alone."

"Yeah, come on," said Marv. "Open up. It's Santa and his elf."

Kevin crawled along the kitchen floor and stuck the barrel of the BB gun out though Ralphy's doggie door. Meanwhile Harry banged on the door again.

"We ain't gonna hurt you," he said.

"Yeah," said Marv. "We got some nice presents for you."

"And I've got a present for you," Kevin whispered as he aimed the BB gun at Harry's knee and squeezed the trigger. *Pop!*

"Yeow!" Harry grabbed his knee and jumped away. Marv bent down and stuck his face in the doggie door to see what had happened.

Pop! Pop! Pop! Kevin shot him in the forehead.

"Eeesshh!" Marv rolled away from the door, clutching his forehead. "The kid's armed!"

"Split up," Harry said. "I'll go around the front. You go in the basement." He started limping away.

Inside, Kevin ran toward the front door with the blowtorch. If everything went right, he wouldn't have to worry about the guy in the basement for awhile.

Marv's forehead throbbed. He snuck around to the cellar door and started down the concrete steps. *Whoops! Bang! Thud!* A moment later Marv found himself lying at the bottom of the steps. They were solid ice. His back was killing him, but he got up, grabbed the crowbar and cracked the basement door open.

It was dark inside. Marv slowly felt his way along the wall for a light switch. He saw something hanging from the ceiling. Great. A light bulb with a chain. He grabbed the chain and pulled. *Crunk!* The chain, bulb and socket came loose in his hand. Suddenly Marv heard a loud metallic clatter. What the . . . ? He looked up and *thunk!* An iron fell down the laundry chute and hit him right in the face.

Meanwhile, Harry scampered toward the front porch. This is gonna be easy, he thought. Marv would go in the back and he'd go in the front. There was no way the kid could stop them.

Harry stepped onto the porch and immediately slipped and fell on his face. "What the . . . ?"

The whole porch was solid ice. Wait a minute, Harry thought. He'd been on this same porch just three days ago. There was no ice then and it hadn't rained since. The kid must've iced the porch!

"Wait till I get my hands on you," Harry mumbled as he held onto a pillar for balance and slowly pulled himself up. The front doorknob was just a foot away.

Inside Kevin held the torch on the doorknob. It was starting to glow red.

Outside Harry grabbed the doorknob. "Aaahhhhh!" The next thing he knew he was flying backward. *Thunk!* He hit the porch hard again. His hand felt like it was on fire and he pressed it against the ice. *Hissss!* As his scorched hand cooled, leaving a five-finger impression in the ice, Harry stared at the front door. What was going on?

Inside Kevin ran to the kitchen and placed

the torch in the next booby trap. These guys hadn't seen anything yet.

In the basement Marv slowly regained conciousness. It was the kid, he thought. The kid had set up the iron. He'd probably iced the cellar steps, too. Marv's head throbbed with pain. He slowly got up.

He found the steps up into the house. In the dark he didn't see the roofing tar. He took a step. His foot stuck. What now? He looked down. Tar? Marv laughed. That dumb kid thought tar was going to stop him? Just watch. Marv stepped out of his right boot. On the next step he stepped out of his left boot. He left his socks on the next two steps. Big deal. That kid was gonna learn it took more than tar to stop Marv Murchens.

There was one step left. Marv stepped . . . right on the nails Kevin had left for him.

"Ahhhhhh!" Marv grabbed his foot and lost his balance. He fell down the stairs. Backward.

Clutching his burned hand, Harry crawled across the icy porch to the front door and jimmied it open with the crowbar. He crawled into the house and stood up.

"Okay, kid, this is where the tide turns," he yelled angrily. No one answered, but Harry knew the kid was there. Probably in the kitchen with the BB gun. The kitchen door was closed. Harry slowly pushed it open. The wire connected to the blowtorch pulled tight.

Whoosh! A blue-and-orange flame shot out

and Harry's hair burst into flames. A second later a fireball shot through the living room and out the front door. *Hissss!* Harry pressed his burning head onto the porch and melted some more ice.

Kevin watched the whole thing from the top of the stairs. "See what happens to hotheads?" he yelled.

Marv finished pulling the nails out of his foot just about the same time Harry lifted his singed head from the icy porch. This is war, they both thought furiously. If two grown crooks couldn't take a seven-year-old kid, they didn't belong in the profession. Harry charged back through the front door just as Marv burst into the living room.

"Where are you, twerp?" Harry shouted.

"I'm here, Harry," shouted Marv.

"Not you, the kid!" yelled Harry. He looked around the dark foyer. "It's too late for you, kid! We're comin' for ya!"

"Great!" Kevin called back. "Come and get me."

Harry stormed into the kitchen and straight into a sheet of Saran Wrap covered with epoxy glue. As he pulled it off his face, he heard a whirring noise and turned around. A fan started to turn, blowing a pile of pillow feathers at him.

"Oh, no!" Harry yelled. But it was too late.

Marv heard Harry's cry and started toward the kitchen. In his path were a dozen little

Christmas ornaments made of the thinnest glass imaginable. And Marv wasn't wearing shoes.

"Yaaaahhhhhh!" he screamed.

At the top of the stairs Kevin smiled and picked up his BB gun. Things were going well.

A few moments later Harry bumped into Marv in the living room. Harry was still pulling feathers out of his eyes. Marv was pulling glass from the bottoms of his feet.

"Why'd you take off your shoes?" Harry asked.

"Why'd you set your head on fire?" Marv replied.

"You guys give up yet?" Kevin shouted.

Harry and Marv stared at each other.

"I can't believe the kid's taunting us," Harry said.

"Where is he?" Marv asked. "I'm gonna murder that kid."

"I'm at the top of the stairs," Kevin yelled.

Both crooks dashed into the foyer, where Kevin had left his Micromachines neatly lined up.

"Aaaaahhhhhh!" *Crash!* Both crooks went flying. Kevin aimed the BB gun and started firing.

"Hey, stay still," he yelled. "It's not easy hitting moving targets."

"I'll kill him!" Harry shrieked. The crooks jumped to their feet and headed for the stairs. They were so enraged they hardly felt the BBs Kevin was firing.

But Kevin had something they would feel. Old paint cans. Full of paint.

Marv saw the first can coming and ducked. It hit Harry right in the face and knocked him back down the stairs. While Marv watched his buddy hit the floor, Kevin threw the second paint can. It hit Marv in the head. A moment later both crooks lay still on the floor. Kevin sat at the top of the stairs.

"This is the way Christmas Eve should be," he said. "Nice and quiet."

DECEMBER 24
OAK PARK
10 P.M.

Harry opened his eyes. He was lying at the bottom of the steps. Every part of his body throbbed with pain and his mouth felt different.

Next to him, Marv moved and groaned. "I don't get it. He's only a kid."

"Shut up," Harry mumbled as he got on his hands and knees.

"Hey, Harry?" Marv said. "You're missing some teeth."

"Well, you're missing some brains," Harry said. "Now let's get that kid. I'm gonna grind him into hamburger."

Upstairs Kevin heard them and his eyes went wide with fear. He'd hoped that after the paint can bombing the crooks would give up. If they actually came up the stairs he didn't have many booby traps left.

Kevin had to make a quick decision. He knew the police wanted him for toothbrush theft, but wouldn't it be better to spend time in jail than be ground into a hamburger? He ran into his mother's room and quickly dialed 911.

"Oak Park police department."

"Listen," Kevin whispered. "My house is being robbed. I live on Rivard Street. The house number's one, one, three — "

Before he could finish he heard the steps creak. The crooks were coming up the stairs!

"You throw another can, kid," Harry shouted. "And I'll boil you in oil *before* I grind you into hamburger."

"One, one, three what?" the switchboard operator asked. But Kevin never heard her. He had to get up to the attic.

Just as Kevin crept out of his parents' bedroom, the crooks came down the hall. Harry lunged at him, but hit the wire Kevin had strung through the doorway. Marv fell on top of Harry.

Kevin ran for the attic stairs, but a hand went around his left ankle!

"Help!" Kevin screamed, kicking Marv in the head with his right foot. "Help! Help!"

Marv held tight and tried to fend off Kevin's kicks. He wasn't about to let this kid go now.

"Come on, Harry!" he shouted. "Get up. Grab him!"

But Harry didn't move. He was lying on the floor pinned under Marv. His eyes were open wide with horror because on the floor about a foot away, racing toward him was . . . Axl the tarantula!

Axl jumped on Harry's face.

"Whhaaaa!" Harry jumped up, throwing Marv off him. Kevin broke free and ran for the attic stairs. Harry peeled the spider off his face and threw it . . . right into Marv's face! Marv pulled the spider off. Axl started to run across the floor. Harry grabbed the crowbar and swung at Axl. Instead he hit Marv in the shin. Marv grabbed the crowbar and started to swing it at Harry.

"Wait!" Harry shouted.

"What?" Marv shouted back.

"Who are we fighting?"

Marv looked at Harry, then at the crowbar, then at Kevin, who was climbing the attic stairs. "Get him!"

They ran up into the attic. Twenty feet away, Kevin stood next to the open attic window, trying to catch his breath. The metal hook was lodged in the windowsill and the escape rope already hung down off the roof.

The crooks grinned at him. The one who'd gotten burned had no hair left on his head and gaps in his mouth where his teeth used to be. The one who still had hair was limping on his shredded feet.

"Dead end, kid," Harry said with a nasty smile. "Now where you gonna go?"

"Yeah," said Marv. "Before we were just

gonna kidnap you. Now we're gonna kidnap you and feed you to the fishes."

"Fish don't like hamburger," Kevin said. "And besides, you guys can go kiss a dog on the lips."

The crooks looked at each other.

"Can I shoot him?" Marv asked. "Please?"

"Sure," said Harry. "Right after I strangle him."

Kevin dove out the window.

"Hey!" Harry shouted.

Kevin quickly climbed to the edge of the roof. He could see his breath. It was cold out. His tree house was in the shadows one story down. Kevin grabbed the rope and started to lower himself toward the big oak branch the tree house sat on.

Harry stuck his head out the window. All he could see was the rope disappearing off the edge of the roof.

"Where'd he go?" Marv asked.

"I don't know. Maybe he committed suicide."

"I'm down here, you big jerk," Kevin yelled from his tree house. "Come and get me before I call the police!"

In the attic Marv turned and limped back toward the stairs.

"Come on!" he shouted at Harry.

"Wait!" Harry yelled.

Marv stopped. "What?"

"That's exactly what he wants us to do," Harry said. "Go back down through his fun house and get tore up again."

"If we don't he'll call the cops!" Marv argued.

Harry pulled a bandana out of his pocket and wrapped it around his scorched hand.

"You're not goin' out the window," Marv gasped.

"It's the last thing the kid expects," Harry said. "Now come on."

Kevin squatted in the tree house and watched Harry crawl to the edge of the roof and start to lower himself down the rope. Marv followed behind him.

"Boy, these guys are dumb," Kevin whispered as he picked up his father's hedge trimmers. He waited until the two crooks had slid down the rope past the tree house. Then he crawled out on the branch.

"Hey, guys," Kevin said with a smile as he opened the hedge cutters. The two crooks looked up at him with horrified expressions on their faces. They were still two stories off the ground. Kevin started to close the hedge cutters on the rope.

"Uh, kid," Harry said. "Let's make a deal. Suppose we just go — "

"Down," Kevin said as he closed the hedge trimmers.

Whomp! Whomp! Two crooks bounced against the side of the house and hit the ground.

A second later Kevin climbed out of the tree. Nearby the crooks lay in a pile. That had to be the end for them. They'd been through more agony in one night than Kevin had been through in his whole life. And these guys didn't have four brothers and sisters dumping on them either.

Then one of the crooks started to move. Kevin couldn't believe it. These guys took more abuse than Wile E. Coyote took from the Road Runner! Kevin looked around. It was no use going back into his house. He'd used up all his booby traps. He had to find a phone to call the police. Where could he go? The only person home on the block was old man Marley.

Kevin raced across the street. As he reached old man Marley's front lawn he looked back and saw the two crooks hobbling after him. Kevin rounded the front corner of the house and headed for the backyard. In the dark he saw the cellar steps.

Real . . . dead . . . bodies! Buzz's words rang in his ears. Kevin stopped. What if his brother was right?

"No," Kevin whispered. "You can't believe that stuff any more. From now on you have to act like a grown-up."

Or at least a teenager.

He let himself into old man Marley's cellar and stopped to hear if there was anyone upstairs, but his heart was beating so hard all he could hear was *thump, thump, thump.* It was dark and shadowy, but across the cellar he saw steps leading up into the house.

Kevin quickly ran up the steps and yanked open the door. And froze.

The crooks were standing there. They were so banged-up they looked like escapees from a refugee camp, but they were grinning.

"You got in the front door?" Kevin gasped.

Harry nodded and grinned. With his missing teeth and swollen hairless head, he reminded Kevin of a jack-o'-lantern.

Kevin trembled and took a step back, but he knew there was no escape. He'd never get out of the cellar alive. He was about to become . . . hamburger.

Harry reached toward the kid. He was going to enjoy making him scream. And this empty house was the perfect place. No one would hear it.

Then someone tapped him on the shoulder.

"Not now, Marv," Harry said. "I want to savor this."

"What are you talking about?" Marv asked.

Harry stopped. "Didn't you just tap me on the shoulder?"

"No."

"Then who . . . ?" Harry turned around. A wide metal snow shovel was swinging toward his head. *BRANNNGGG!* It made contact and Harry sank to the floor.

Marv spun around. The snow shovel was now headed for him. *BRONNGGG!* Marv hit the floor beside Harry.

Kevin looked up, astonished. "Mr. Marley?"

Old man Marley stepped out of the shadows. "How's my aim?"

"Good, Mr. Marley," Kevin grinned. "Really good."

A little while later Kevin and old man Marley stood in the driveway and watched the cops put the crooks in the back of their patrol car.

"Those guys have been hanging around the neighborhood for a couple of days," Kevin told one of the policemen. "You might want to check if any of the houses around here have been robbed."

"How'd they get so banged up?" the cop asked Kevin.

"They must be really clumsy," Kevin said. The cop nodded and got into his patrol car.

"How about some hot chocolate?" old man Marley asked.

"Thanks," Kevin said. "But I have a lot of cleaning up to do."

"On Christmas Eve?" Old man Marley looked surprised.

"Yeah," said Kevin. "Santa's bringing me a big surprise."

December 25: Christmas Day
Oak Park
8 A.M.

Kevin woke up and looked out the window. It had snowed during the night! The whole neighborhood was covered with a beautiful blanket of white. He jumped out of bed and shot down the stairs. A white Christmas! This was great! No way Santa was going to let him down. His family was going to be right there in the —

Kevin skidded to a stop in the living room. The presents he'd wrapped were still under the Christmas tree. The room was empty.

"Mom?" Kevin said.

No one answered. Kevin couldn't believe it. The whole struggle against the crooks . . . everything he'd cleaned up for . . . the way he'd acted so grown-up . . . it was all for nothing because that bum Santa didn't deliver.

"Darn!" Kevin was so mad and disappointed he picked up a crystal paperweight from the coffee table. He'd show Santa. He'd wreck that tree with one throw. Kevin pulled his arm back, ready to heave the paperweight . . . but he couldn't do it. Why wreck the tree? That was the old Kevin. The kid who couldn't do anything for himself. The kid who was always a pain because it was the only way he could get attention.

Besides, maybe it wasn't Santa's fault. The guy was supposed to bring gifts, not bodies.

Kevin slowly climbed the stairs back to his parents' bedroom. It was his fault. He never should've wished his family would disappear. It served him right that he had to spend Christmas Day alone. And if he had to spend it alone, he might as well spend it in bed.

A snow-covered station wagon with a tuba strapped to the roof pulled into the driveway.

"Here ya are, Mrs. McCallister," Gus said. "Home safe and sound."

"Gus, I don't know how I'll ever thank you." Kate leaned over and gave him a kiss on the cheek.

"You could be the first person in Oak Park to buy our record," Gus said. "The 'I Don't Want Her You Can Take Her, She Can't Stuff the Kielbasa Polka.' "

Kate promised she would and waved as the station wagon backed out of the driveway. Then she walked to the front door and took out her key. She was thankful the house was still standing. Now if only Kevin was safe.

She opened the door and peeked in. Something was wrong. The house was so . . . clean! Kevin couldn't possibly be there. Worried, she stepped into the living room, but stopped when she saw the Christmas tree. It was only two-and-a-half-feet tall.

How sweet! He'd put up a tree with decorations and gifts underneath! Kate could tell he'd done it all himself. The carrots were a dead giveaway. Her concern melted away to pure happiness and she felt her eyes brimming with tears. But where was Kevin? If he was there Kate knew how to find him. She picked up a silver Christmas bell ornament and rang it gently.

Ring, ring, ring. Upstairs Kevin sat on his parents' bed, gazing sadly at the framed portrait of his family.

Ring, ring, ring. He looked up. What was that?

Ring, ring, ring. He went out on the landing, but couldn't see anything. He started down the stairs slowly. One of the steps creaked. At the bottom of the stairs he looked around the foyer, then peeked into the dining room. No one.

Ring, ring, ring. It was behind him. He spun around.

"Mom!" Kevin cried. Her clothes were all wrinkled and her hair was a mess, but he didn't care. Santa had come through after all!

"Merry Christmas, sweetheart," Kate said, rushing toward her little boy, feeling the tears slide down her face. She kneeled down and hugged him. "I'm so sorry we left you."

Kevin hugged her around the neck as hard as he could. "I'm sorry too, Mom. I'll never be a pain again. I promise. And I'll do all the stuff I'm supposed to do, like make my bed and brush my teeth and go to sleep at bedtime."

Kate stared at her son, not quite sure what must have caused this big change. Meanwhile, Kevin was looking around. "Hey, where's everyone else?"

"Oh, hon, they're all still back in — "

Before Kate could finish, the front door opened and Buzz and Megan came in.

"Did you have to fall asleep and drool all over me in the cab?" Buzz asked angrily.

"I don't drool," Megan snapped back.

Linnie and Peter were behind them.

"Will you guys please shut up?" Linnie said.

"Come on, you jerks," said Peter. "It's Christmas . . . hey, Kev!"

Kevin was so glad to see his father, he ran into his arms. Buzz even patted him on the head.

"It's pretty cool you didn't burn the place down," his big brother said.

Meanwhile Kate was amazed to see the rest of her family. "How in the world did you get back here?"

"We got the night flight back," Peter said. "Remember? The one you didn't want to wait for?"

Kate kissed her husband.

"Who wants to get the presents out of the car?" Peter asked. "Jeff, you just volunteered."

"Gimme a break. I haven't even said hello to my brother yet." Jeff turned to Kevin. "Hey, dude, you didn't miss anything. The TV shows were all in French."

"Now go get the presents," Peter ordered.

Jeff went out. Linnie came over and hugged Kevin.

"I'll be the only decent person in the family and say I really, really missed you and worried about you," she said. "But you can't use that against me, okay?"

"Are you saying I didn't miss him?" Megan butted in. "It just so happens I cried several times. And at least once it was for real."

"Don't fight," Kevin said. "Please? Let's all be happy."

His two sisters stared at him. Linnie put her hand on his forehead. "Are you feeling okay?"

"Do you think there's a store open?" Kate asked, thinking about a Christmas celebration. "We used up all the milk before we left."

"I bought some yesterday," Kevin said. "And some eggs and fabric softener, too."

Everyone stared at him.

"*You* went shopping?" Buzz asked in awe.

"What else did you do while we were gone?" asked Linnie.

Kevin thought for a moment. Should he tell them? No, they'd never believe it.

"Mostly I just hung around," he said.

Soon everything was back to normal. Everyone went in a different direction, except Peter, who bent down and picked up something shiny from the floor.

"What's this?" he asked, holding up Harry's gold tooth.

Kevin's jaw dropped. "It's . . . uh, it's . . ."

"Maybe your mother will know." Peter headed for the kitchen.

Kevin let out a big sigh and walked to the living room window. He looked out at the trees covered in white.

"Thanks for bringing back my family, Santa," he whispered. "And thanks for the snow, too."

Across the street a car pulled into old man Marley's driveway. Mr. Marley came out and hugged the man who'd been driving. Then Kevin saw Mr. Marley's granddaughter get out. So the guy Mr. Marley was hugging must've been his son!

"They made up!" Kevin whispered. "All right!"

Suddenly Kevin realized old man Marley was looking at him. Marley smiled and gave Kevin a little wave. Kevin smiled and waved back. Everything had worked out perfectly! Boy, this really was a merry Christmas.

About the Author

Todd Strasser has written many award-winning novels for young and teenaged readers. He is a frequent speaker at junior and senior high schools, and conferences. He lives in New York City with his wife and children. They usually stay home during the holidays.